How to Leave the World

How to Leave the World

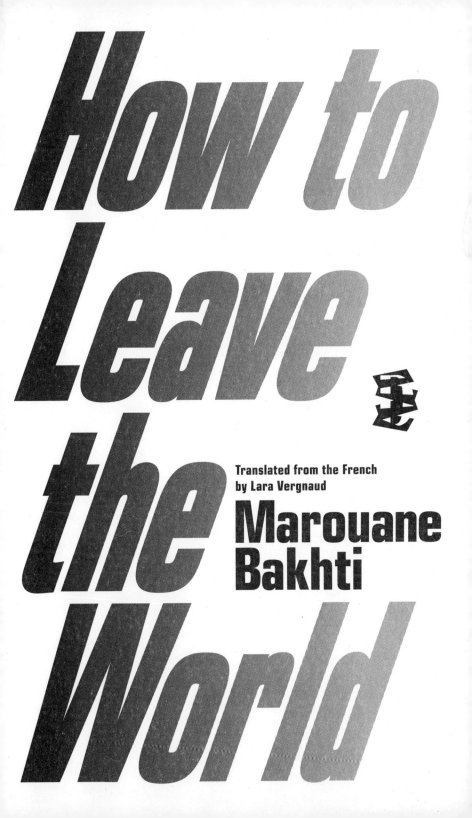

Translated from the French
by Lara Vergnaud

Marouane Bakhti

DIVIDED

This edition published in the United Kingdom by Divided in 2024.

Divided Publishing
Rue de Manchesterstraat 5
1080 Brussels
Belgium

Divided Publishing
Deborah House
Retreat Place
London E9 6RJ
United Kingdom

https://divided.online

Originally published in Paris in 2023 by Les Nouvelles Éditions du Réveil
as *Comment sortir du monde*.

Designed by Alex Walker
Printed by Printon, Tallinn

ISBN 978-1-7395161-3-0

Under the Willow Trees

Lust in my heart, I wanted to leave at any cost. Leave the ugliness, leave the gloomy patches of green amid vast expanses of grey. I wanted to destroy everything, take the country out of the boy and vice versa, abandon the sexual wasteland I had wandered for so long. *Au revoir* and *adieu*.

And yet that was where my child-self learned what makes a tree a tree and how to cradle a newborn animal in his hands.

I can see myself, disgusted with all of them, along the flat route the bus would take. The tragedy of not seeing another creature like me, anywhere.

The vastness of that suburban sprawl, doomed to a wild unharmony, still takes centre stage in my memory.

A boy at the edge of a field full of livestock, barbed wire against my legs.

My heart is a copse of trees filled with black stones, the looming terror of being caught red-handed in desire.
My heart is a copse of trees filled with shark's teeth, the ones my father brought me back from the desert.
And beneath the skin of slowworms, I sense eggs ready to hatch.

The long living-room sofa, its leather cracked by naps, that hosts my unending inner vociferations. The narrow house facing the willows and the birches that sing in the wet wind. The table in the dining room that opens onto a garden of weeds, thistles and mole holes.

My lip bleeding from his rough hand. The blow softened by the taste of dates. In the afternoons, I daydream on the cold white tiles. Cats coming and going through the windows. Bright light everywhere in the house.

I believe in meteorites and I look for them in the loose soil of the undergrowth. I believe in the miracle of God and I look for it in the loose soil of the undergrowth.

These are the only memories left in my mind, they write themselves. I don't know why they're all I see when I shut my eyes. The wonder and torment of a childhood spent hiding.

I think about the forest hemmed in by roads, and in which there was still some wildlife left. I used to like talking to the animals. Carcasses of Eid sheep through the branches and insect wings that could make you believe in fairies.

That's how I remember it. Chasing woodland ghosts and burying my shame.

Yesterday, I had a long conversation with a friend who told me, 'It's also good *not* to hate your past.'

So then I told her, 'The place I was born is utterly incapable of preparing us for the world. The place that brought me into being kills your dreams and swallows your hopes. It's completely flat, bleak with a few green spots.'

I can still see them. Groups of boys in plastic clothes (meanwhile my mother was dressing me in corduroy and khaki cotton). They would look at me and with their light-coloured eyes, faces already puffy with fatigue, say: 'We couldn't tell you why, but you're our enemy. You're our enemy for a thousand reasons that are no longer true. Reasons that are no longer true for us or for our parents.'

For a long time I couldn't stand the sight of them. In my memories I spit at them. They're bullying me and meanwhile I'm looking at my parents, an Arab and a local girl, and I don't understand why they chose to subject us to this. Thankfully, there's the gentle countryside. There are the spinneys and the marshes that connect them. But there's no escaping the boys on mopeds, in front of the school, at the port, in the streets of the housing estates I roam alone on my bright-red BMX.

My friend is listening. I tell her how I was able to forgive them. I tell her the whole story. The place where I grew up is a swampland.

It's true. It's a lake surrounded by swamps. It's a world of vague, jumbled rivalries. I never knew where my allies were. I didn't understand why people were mistrustful, why they looked at my father the way that they did. And amid the picking of sides and gleeful childish taunts, the main lesson: Arabs, faggots, we hate them both!

The long horizon of cream-coloured brick houses is interrupted by fields, and in the fields, beige cows coated in dry mud.

The locals don't understand why it's the town Arabs who have the nicest car. The locals would hate for anyone to think they work the land like that family on the side of the road.

It's a lake surrounded by swamps, but it's also a large wet plain gashed by strips of black and grey asphalt that allow cars to inundate the shopping centres and their car parks.

Massive car parks, all that energy (all those hands) it took to squash the green and cover it with tarmac. All that energy that could have produced something remarkable, something beautiful. The best schools. Gardens brimming with fruit. Huge mansions for dancing in, knocking back Heinekens, playing drinking games and racing dirt bikes.

This is what I'm daydreaming as I wait for my mother and her full trolley to emerge from the shopping tower erected amid the cement. She comes out of Leclerc, sunglasses on her nose. Sometimes I don't wait for her outside. I go into the supermarket with her and sit on the cold, stained tiles across from the magazine racks. I skim through *National Geographic*: snow leopards and a sale on Bonnin brioches over the loudspeaker. I invent exotic worlds. I love visiting the fridge in the fishing aisle and watching the pink and yellow maggots in their plastic boxes. They wriggle slowly, stiff from the cold. I look for life at the fish counter. I touch the unmoving animals displayed on a bed of ice in front of a woman in a hairnet who never smiles. I imagine stealing the crabs in the aquarium behind her and releasing them in the brooks behind our garden. I'm looking for something to save.

I can picture myself perfectly on the way home, silent, head leaning against the car door.

There's a path that goes from the top of the street and leads straight into the pastures. The concrete is crumbling, it forms a clay that mixes with roots and fallen leaves.

The street that goes past our front door is lined with detached homes, and at the end, the fishing spot.

The catfish of my childhood are there.
    The writhing on the pebbly ground in a puddle of mucus and sludge and bubbles is there.
    The fishermen crushing tiny skulls with their boots are there.
    My grief and the few flatheaded fish that I could return to the pond, their barbels snagging on my palm, are there.

And also, the fluorescent green line that plunges into the brown water, and the sun beating down on me, the dog and the willow trees.

My father tries to mirror the local men – Sundays are for fishing. I watch him, I get bored.

The only miracle is when I can grab the bulging fish, so gelatinous and sticky. They stiffen beneath my fingers.
     The smell is terrible, but my morbid fascination for their frantic out-of-water struggle keeps me awake on the stone bench.

I would watch herons and egrets take flight in a sky forever filled with clouds. My fears, too, took wing. Of being with other people but not only; having to walk with them, talk with them, laugh with them.

As a teenager, I go back to sit on the white stone bench but it's no longer a refuge. It's wet and reeks of dead fish.

I see animals all around me, all kinds of animals. I think about their burrows at the base of trees. I catch them and hold tightly with both hands.

They tremble like leather bags of bones.
     The rabbits have eyes full of hard balls that might fall out of their skulls, those eyes visible beneath two long ears lined with blue and red blood vessels.

My mother tries to stop us, but for my brother and me the ability to catch and touch the animals is too exciting. When we're bored, we invariably find something stupid to do and sometimes those stupid things turn out to be a bit cruel.
     One day, my mother said, 'It's myxomatosis . . .'

I don't think I understood that it was something serious, that it was a disease. I can still feel the fear growing inside me, alongside disgust.

And at dawn, the veil of fog over the garden, the trees' winter skeletons poking through, emaciated rabbits inching forward and nibbling the frost-tipped grass. They advance slowly like ghosts from hell. Like the jinn of my bedtime stories, disembodied animals floating across the frozen white ground.

One day, the morning light no longer revealed their tiny bodies eaten away by sickness.

My mother said, 'It's over. The disease ran its course at last . . .'

There are dead rabbits and dragonflies whose wings I grab with two fingers. Red and blue, they look like robots with iridescent jointed bodies.

There's the dirt I play with. Clay I use to mould creatures. I sculpt animal heads from the mud. I set up strange displays on tree stumps, deformed faces and bizarre bodies against the moss. Large horns and sharpened beaks, a bizarre pantheon created just for me.

I let my monsters dry in the August sun before placing them below the trees, returning them to the forest.

And then there's my mother's voice penetrating the trunks and summoning me from my round hut of willow and hazel branches, like a large bark dome. That's where I nap, and where I hear her calling me.

I spend all my time in the forest, only taking breaks for lunch or dinner.

Hidden in the branches, I keep watch for the blue tit, the great tit, the hoopoe and the thrush. I trap them using shoeboxes and as I hold them in my hands, I watch red lice run through their feathers. I touch their eyes so I can feel their thin eyelids close. I release them quickly, before their small hearts explode from the forced proximity to my human features, my human smell, my fingers, my human gargantuanism.

There's the flock and the births.
Once a year, lambs emerge from the ewes' bulging bellies in red and yellow liquids.
A tiny hop into the world.
Some remain stretched out on the grass and never bleat.

The mothers are distraught: their babies are dead.

It's true, there's the flock and animals dying.

An apple-green Beyblade spinning-top in my hand, it's time for the sacrifice and I'm morose.

As a child, I never watch the throats being slit because I'm deathly afraid of blood.

It's the ceremony that follows that I memorised.

Large blades that slice tendons and clip nails.

Sounds ringing in the garage, I slip my head through the half-open door.

I see: a suspended body. It's my beloved lamb.
I see: their mouths blowing air under the wool with a hose, inflating the animal.
And I see: their hands tugging off the fleece, like a skin being sloughed.

Then it's time to remove the fatty layer that makes such a pleasing noise when the skin detaches, using another large knife, and reveal pink flesh that still has streaks of white fat across the muscles. The entrails are removed in one disgusting dump. I see lungs for the first time, then a heart, then a kidney.

Now, every time someone tells me about a health issue in this or that part of their body, I visualise the detached sheep organs from when I was five.

Then they leave the animal to rest, still hanging from its hind legs.

Dragon Metal Fusion between my fingers and blue Nikes all the way from Morocco, a windbreaker and corduroy trousers ripped at the knees.

Dragonfly larvae in the stream leave tiny bitemarks on the tips of my fingers.

I go deep into the small forest. There are three of them.

A little blood, barely a puddle, beneath the sheep dangling from a hook lodged between tendon and bone.

Between the tree trunks, I see hanging carcasses. They're wrapped in the fitted sheets that my father grabbed without thinking. The ones from my bed, with monsters on them. The cotton is warm to the touch and some of the muscles twitch in a reminder of life. Like a ghost.

It smells of fear and the yellow fat of sheep's wool.
    I stay and contemplate the silence that follows their killing while my uncles drink coffee on the patio.

They're letting the meat rest.

The names I gave the lambs are still in my head.

'It's the most beautiful day of the year.'

I'm not sure. Although it is what God expects of us.

The following day, I go back to watch when it's time to stretch the cooled carcass and break the bones.
I almost always respond to my mother's call, hunger growling in my belly. She pulls me from my contemplation and my catches.

At night I don't want to sit to my father's right, but I do want some of the steaming gratin. I run home, skipping over dead trees and brambles, and enter the house covered with mud and leaves. This time, my mother's voice is hard, she's tired of cleaning up the traces of the outdoors that I spread about inside. Tiny branches in my bed, thistles on my socks.

I love the trees that surround me, just like my jeddi loved them. He used to graft them, wedding prune trees and pear trees, for example. It worked well, the end result beautiful. Spring was a time of joy for him. He would go from trunk to trunk, cutting to cutting, to check whether his little projects had succeeded. Limping slightly on his crutch, with a smile or furrowed brow, he'd call us over, '*Aji!* Have a look at this. It's a fig tree bud.' Or: '*Shouf*, this here's a disease. The plant won't survive.'

One day I brought him a little field mouse whose hindquarters were paralysed. I hoped that he would help me, that we would save it together. He told me, 'This animal's already dead.' I thought him cruel. The tiny rodent lasted a few more days, dehydrated and infected. There was nothing I could do. Before the utter powerlessness of my age, he didn't console me. He didn't know how to do that kind of thing.

I do remember, however, that we ate huge black cherries from his tree. I remember that we abundantly watered his vegetable garden come nightfall and fed the lambs in the shack.

That was his remedy, the plaster for my pain, a simple idea in the end: the understanding of what we experience for what it is. A slow cycle that always ends up giving back what was taken.

I spent a lot of time in those branches, hanging, sitting high as I could so I wouldn't drown in the noise and fervour of celebrations and endless dinners.

I'm in collusion with the trees now that they've become political. I smile when I see how obsessed city people are with the artificial versions planted in cement. It's the ideology around them, which means nothing to the trees, that I find amusing. That said, obviously there's nothing to be gained by not planting actual forests in the city. Roots and branches everywhere to remind me, always, of the past.

During the day, if you follow the path that leads past the house and melts into the countryside, there are people out walking. There are their mad dogs panting with joy.

And at night: the headlights shining away from the trees reveal nothing but brown road and the surrounding emptiness.

I see his Airness jacket on the ground, covered in mud. His taste and smell stayed with me for a long time. The freckles on his skin and his thick red body hair. We met up a couple of times like that, behind the brand-new moped. It lasted a few weeks at the most. He was the first one to put his dick deep inside me.

He would show up on his shiny black machine in the night that protected him and gave us the impression we were just playing make-believe. No one knew that we were in the habit of meeting up to smoke stolen cigarettes in the hunters' cabin. A few planks of wood and an asphalt roof. He always had cans of *panaché* in the top box of his moped. He had burn marks on his hands. When he dropped his joggers, our synthetic boxers were already wet, even before he came on me. He'd make me come and then he'd go again. He didn't say much. He told me how he got the deep purple scar that went from the top of his forehead to the corner of his mouth, skipping his left eye — a dog that broke its chain even though it had been wound three times around a caravan wheel. He doesn't know what became of the dog. I tell him about the sheep, my beloved sheep that were turned into scraps of meat.

Our trainers digging into a floor of twigs and rifle cartridges. Hooks to hang dead animals on, a large flat table for us to lie down on.

That tiny world is where silence mounted its high walls around my desire. We weren't very far from my family's house. Our refuge was a fixed part of the ecosystem: the woods, the inhabited road, the deserted road, the lake and its swamps.

My secret germinates between my ribs and plunges its roots into the surrounding marshes. It wants to come out, it wants to be born, and as I grow up, I crush it somewhere on the bottom. But then the lie drinks the muddy water, it's thirsty, it grows and grows, it swells with no end in sight. It takes up all the space in my mind. I'm terrified at the idea that someone might find out what everyone already knows.

When I remember my unhappiness as a teenager, I picture the road that leads down to the lake and think: a no-man's land. At the end of the summer, A. leaves me. He stops answering my messages. The forest doesn't seem so beautiful anymore.

The undergrowth where we loved each other, where we pretended not to love each other, continues from the lake to the garden of my house, forming a loop.

I grow up in this shapeless place on the path to a progress and prosperity that never materialise. Modernity came and killed all the old forms of knowledge. It pulled up the ancestral roots, then, boom, it levelled the woodlands, ripped up the country-side, in need of ever more motorways.

And yet, the boys remain. The boys became men, got married, and constructed what they call 'pavilions'. Which is just a fancy word for detached houses.

Most of them thought it was fine, that it was normal. Most of them thought that I was the problem and not the tremendous isolation and fear of everything that had made them so brutal.

Most of them saw us as a threat when my strange family moved to town.

And meanwhile I can't just sit here and stay quiet, can't force myself to like girls and race across the pitch with the boys. I can't do it and they make me pay. I don't hate them anymore for it, really, I don't. Often I find myself crying, wishing I had been even gentler with them, even more docile with all of those boys on motorbikes cackling with laughter when they saw my body in my absurd clothes and my delicate hands free of cigarette stains. And their conversations from which I was always excluded.

While they're shoulder-barging, digging their studs into each other's reddened calves, ripping off their opponents' plastic shin pads mid-tackle, I'm in the middle of the football pitch playing with worms. Games usually start early on Saturdays, when the night-crawlers are still making their way across the pitch. I don't want them to be trampled to death.

It's also, for example, the story of their fists to my head behind the changing-room door.

And my father asking, 'Why don't you like playing sport like all the other boys?'

It's also, for example, their gobs of spit on my new jacket.

And my mother saying, 'Why don't you want to wear your jacket? It's winter, it's freezing outside, all the other girls and boys are wearing theirs . . .'

I grow up with the secret of that rejection. I say, 'Everything's fine.' No one realises the extent of the isolation forced on me. I'm cold without a jacket on the way to school. My slender shoulders hunched over on the gravel path alongside the road, which is dangerous and dark in the morning gloom. I'm cold as I wait at the bus stop.

Then there's another story, the one where I start to feel fond of them. Fond of the hands they secretly dare to run down my body. My mind split in two by the fear of letting them. Terrified of being called out by the same mouths that want to kiss me.

It has to be said: this affection for men appeared amid their violence towards me.

But there were respites and refuges.

Mémé's house smelled like a spice or a flower I've forgotten, that we've all let die in our memories.

The table I never saw, always covered by a soft thick tablecloth. I lay my head on it, and there are crumbs stuck to my face when I wake up. And for that, this remains a place of healing for a long time. Somewhere to recuperate, to let the wounds scab over.

Before she died, obviously. It always comes back to me the same way. I see her tiny body rigid and wizened in her bed. I feel her skin, cold and lifeless, beneath my adult lips.

Every time I cry, it's a grown man's large tears for a small hunched-over woman.

Mémé was wedded to the land, a true *paysanne*. Her hands were broadened by her labours, but soft. She had two beautiful wicker baskets she would use to gather fruit from her garden. I can still see the sheets of newspaper at the bottom. My mother told me, 'The women living in the marshlands would weave those baskets and sell them at the village market.'

A life incomprehensible to me. A life of brutality, work and suspended thoughts. An existence of rising at dawn and rabbits in a hutch.

I can't remember if she noticed that I was different. She was always gentle, though she never touched me between her two embraces, hello and goodbye.

She had paintings and needlepoints that featured dogs, spaniels she would insist, bringing wild birds back to their hunter-masters. She had strange vases and a dolphin that changed colour depending on the humidity and the meteorological conditions, of which we were always informed on that day's visit.

She had purple forget-me-nots in front of her door and a massive orchard.

The barn still smelled of livestock, though she had sold the animals a long time ago. We were terrified of the wasps and hornets in the field, driven mad by all the rotting and fermenting fruit.

In terror, my brother and I would sprint through the trees to the front door with our heads down to avoid the swarm of vespids attracted by the incredible bounty that Mémé no longer had the strength to pick.

Speaking of food, what are we eating?
Soups, oysters at Christmas, boiled milk that overflows in a fragrant foam. The tiny living room that no one ever entered, and her bedroom, in which I must once have set foot seeing as I have this image in my mind: a bed in walnut, a wardrobe in oak, floral sheets.

Mémé lived through war, both of them, but I have no idea how. She couldn't have been all that afraid here, in this region covered by water.

I never knew what Mémé was afraid of.

One day, towards the end of the end, I put my headphones in her downy ears and turned on the music. And her face . . . Mémé had never heard such a thing before. The world was turning without her and that was fine by her. She never saw the sea, though it wasn't very far away.

I never knew Pépé. He used to hit things when rage took over his thoughts (same as me) and I know that he suffered from the war trapped inside his head, but that's about it.

I wonder if I care?
　　I wonder to what extent these memories of France, the real one, are a part of me.

I almost wrote: the France that lived in the fields, that lived before our century, that I see in textbook photos.

Pitchfork in hand, sitting on bales of hay. That was his life.

The France with icons above the bed. The France that's hidden in the twists and turns in the back of my mind, in the labyrinthine thoughts about my skin colour and my *gwer* accent that gives me away, that reveals I'm not all Arab. So yes, okay, Mémé is a part of me.

Jesus contorting in pain against the wallpaper. The Virgin Mary all in pink overlooking a fireplace out of use since the arrival of electric heating. I felt only slightly concerned by those strange symbols. I didn't truly understand the gold cross around Mémé's neck.

I can't remember if she noticed that I was different. I'm guessing she did.

Mémé never said anything bad about Arabs.
    Mémé would touch my sister's long hair, and remain silent.
    Mémé never offered me charcuterie.

I can't remember if she noticed that I was different.

When we went on long walks in the Vendée, I would run ahead so I didn't have to listen to her stories.

Mémé was fond of my father, she respected him, I think. She had an idea of how men should be, and women. So she must have noticed that I was different . . . I can't remember.

She never came to visit us. We always went to her, to her little house with the low ceiling, filled with that smell missing from our memories. She was too tired to come to us.

Off to Mémé's house, off the beaten path, where you can finally catch your breath. After we leave, stuffed, we return to our regular family life that bristles with impatience.

And my other family: an insatiable vortex populated by aunts and uncles, all of whom are short-tempered, all of whom are tender. And then, hours spent roaming the garden, discovering my solitude. Frenzied excitement and intermittent silences beneath the trees.
    I don't do much inside the house, with my cousin M. Every once in a while we dress up.

We wrap dusters and sheets around ourselves, cinched at the waist, and we're transformed into icons and statues. We steal my sister's red velvet dresses. Now, I'm sitting sidesaddle on the rocking horse. On our heads tower ornate headdresses of towels and pillowcases.

Sometimes, someone will open the door and surprise us in the act, small inventive creatures in high heels. Usually they don't say anything except 'Dinner time,' 'M., your dad's here,' or 'Keep it down.' These are glorious, unprecedented moments of freedom in a time dominated by what grown-ups tell us. Boys must follow the rules. They should dream, of course, of becoming men. Boys mustn't sit around doing nothing. They should be with other boys, running and fighting. Boys are not allowed to wear their mothers' clothes. But here's the big mystery. They decide not to look. They decide to let us play.

Liberated of our shame – *hshouma*, we call it – we gleefully squeeze paper corsets around our skinny bodies.

I liked to spy through trees or from behind doorways. They called me the 'satellite dish'.

I had the habit – 'surprising in a boy,' my aunts always said – of curling up on a *sedari* or a leather couch and then doing absolutely nothing. Wait for the women to start talking. For them to quote their parents, or share something bad they heard about the neighbours. These women support each other through situations that are barely articulated, even among themselves, things whispered, silent complicity. I would study them diligently. I would devote entire afternoons to the conversations of outraged women and resigned women.

I can still picture, through the window, my cousins' faces flushed from exertion, yelling for me to join them. But I stayed inside, limp on the sofa, my arms or knees contorted into impossible positions. This habit taught me a great deal about the interpersonal dynamics of my family. I never said anything to anyone, but I committed all those scraps of truth, the partial revelations, the scandals, true and otherwise, to memory.

Today, with the licence of age, I still see, on my uncles' face, echoes of those whispered conversations. All those tiny key moments that make me understand what fuels my hatred and undying affection for the men in my life.

A glossy geranium tree in front of the house. The flowers look plastic. That overwhelming smell when you crush the leaves in your hand.

Everyone's screaming in the back, in the garden. From a distance it's hard to tell if it's from joy. But I'm off on my own. I'm sticking by the house.

I watch the others constantly. I listen, I observe, I am a round antenna that captures the television signal we don't get here. Sometimes tempers flare and that's when everyone goes home.

Angry and crimson from fighting with words. Other times, in my family, you might throw something in someone's face. I inherited my father's irrational, uncontainable rage. An eruption in the throat.

Lose your mind, and a glass goes flying across the table. More often than not it's the secret nestling between my ribs that sparks the fire. I feel so alone.

Nobody speaks to the creature inside me and often it can't bear any more. That's when it forces me to break doors and punch walls.

As usual, they're all sitting or standing around the garden table. There's a massive fire burning, onto which get tossed cardboard boxes and crates. We feed the fire and then we feed ourselves. Meat, lamb, merguez noisily oozing on the grill set on two breeze blocks green with moss.

My aunts serve water, bright-orange Hawaï and then salad. The men chop, butcher. I smash into these roles like they're brick walls. I don't understand what's expected of me, from the men or the women. This is how it works in our family, how we divide things. The binary omnipresent.

As a kid, injustice isn't speaking clearly into my ear yet. It's hard to make out.

We're kings of the forest putting on a performance that plays out beneath the large oak tree and in the burning pink light of day, which is slowly fading. We eat what we want, we race until we're gasping for breath, between every bite even. You should see us. Kids laughing and putting whatever we want in our mouths. You should see that joy, meat juice dribbling down our fingers and grass stains coating our knees.

The sound of hands on stretched darbuka skins once night falls is very loud. A ruckus made by us (Arabs) in a hamlet at the edge of the woods (French). I'm almost frightened by the trees looming in the dark. The fire's reflection draws chimeras on the trunks, and behind the first trees that form a circle around my jubilant family: total blackness.

All of a sudden it's no longer funny when I'm told to sit down and say something in Arabic. I stammer and, like vultures, they pounce on my embarrassed words.

I hear through their laughter: 'That's what happens when you mix . . . Nothing good comes of it . . . There's no way he'll ever be able to speak our language . . .'

I garble a few phrases, cheeks red. They continue in Arabic. Everything becomes opaque. I can't tell if they're still talking about me.

And the others: 'You can see he can't articulate the way we do . . . Get off his back . . . Leave the boy alone . . . Let him run around in the woods . . .'

They go: 'Say *qāf*? Say *ayn*? There, you see . . . He can't . . .'

And the others again: 'It's not a very useful language though, is it? . . . Don't worry, son . . . We're not really speaking Arabic – it's a dialect. Cobbled together. Look how much good it does me to speak it . . . Go on, go and play by the trees . . .'

They offer theories on my otherness out loud: 'He'll never learn Arabic . . . He's too shy . . . He only ever listens to his mother . . .'

Words that flow and scold and lift and soothe in the language that surrounds me all the livelong day, and not once do I manage to formulate an intelligible sentence. Without realising it, surely, they push me to reject the dialect that fills those days. I'm with them and I don't speak the same tongue. Already a stranger to my own.

I haven't forgotten how I abandoned things in my youth: goodbye language that can't be mine.

It's dark in the garden and a big white lamp at the foot of the oak tree illuminates their faces.

Tongues subdued by the darkness tell stories. They tell of the *bled*, they tell stories the way they do back home: from beginning to end. Anyone who doesn't have the gift has to relinquish the privilege.

I absorb the unfamiliar names, the streets I've never seen, the jokes that don't make sense.

I try to complete my education, to fit in by gulping down draughts of family fables.

Like a little sorcerer, as if I can play catch up, except that I was born already behind.

And then there's the challenge of keeping my Arabness alive along with my desires.

The day my eyes were opened is the day my father slapped me because I was wearing my *gandura* like a strapless dress.

All at once, I became his beloved son and his suspect son. He began observing me, attentive to any traits or gestures that might result in an intolerable version of masculinity. My hair had to be very short, shaved in fact. No more locks dangling over my forehead. I cried when I saw my kiss curls on the floor of the hairdressers at the shopping centre. My movements had to be monitored, along with the intonation of my voice, the way I sat or laughed. And then it became more than just my father, there were all the men and boys in front of whom I tried to camouflage everything that came naturally.

By this rationale, he makes me do sport.

I remember football. I remember the pain.

I remember the changing rooms.

I can still smell the shame and taste the sweat on my tongue when the anxiety returns. I will always smell the dampness of the pitch and feel their boots clanging against my bones.

Then, he tried to teach me Arabic.

I remember being afraid to pronounce the words that filled my entire mouth. I remember being very mean.

I remember making fun of *his* culture.

I remember conflating *his* culture and rage, *his* culture and the hand that flies too swiftly to the back of my head. I think I remember my white mother who wants to keep her son to herself. I see myself conflating everything and thinking that if she makes my life gentler and he makes it more violent, it's because of his culture.

Then he taught me the *shahada*, and it turned out I loved it.

For a while, I thought that I could be the religious member of the family. So I prayed every night. I imagined God as an enormous tower of rocks overlooking the earth, offering humans shade or crushing them beneath landslides.

And then my cousins slept over one Saturday night. I remember them laughing hysterically at my ridiculous gestures, my disorderly, incorrect prayer. I found out that my father was a counterfeit Muslim. He didn't know how to pray. He was the only one in the family who couldn't pray. Father like son and son like father.

I should have guessed. And yet there was the occasional eruption of the sacred in our heathen lives. My father reminding us that you don't waste bread, that it's a gift from God.

Then he gave me a book and I read it. It was easy, pleasant. I remember I started reading a lot. I deliberately bought twice as many books as my sister.

I remember, as a child, waiting for my father to kiss my shaved head and tell me, 'Very good, keep up the reading.'

I can see him saying that he's proud of me, but always to other people. He's proud of me and my docility.

When the carefreeness came to an end, I went through my teenage crisis like everyone else. Right on schedule. When I heard, 'That's not a thing back home,' I decided that it wasn't my home. I decided to be like the others. Like white people.

My father suddenly became a monster of virility, a monster from an asinine country and a disgusting misogynistic religion. A mythology to be set ablaze.

I wore the clothes I was supposed to, did my hair the way I was supposed to. My father became my scapegoat, the target of my terror of being mixed and undefined, forever trembling.

Most importantly: don't resemble the Arabs who don't resemble me enough. Most importantly, pretend.

Look like a lawyer's son, a boy from the north of the city, and keep them guessing.

I would say, 'My name's not Arab, it's Breton.' I had no shame. I was crude, ridiculous, really. I would straighten my hair and plaster it against my head, nice and neat. I wore striped button-up shirts and the village boys were even more confused about who I was. I told myself that on this side of the divide, with white people, I could be free. I crushed and buried my memories of the garden and the *sedaris*, of Tangiers and Ramadan nights.

I broke things. I spent the night out without telling anyone. I liked being morose, I imagined myself a future intellectual. I did whatever would bring me closer to my mother and said whatever would take me further from the father.

I had my crisis of adolescence just like a white kid, so I could be one too, but mainly to escape the melancholy of being mixed. My father was uprooted but me? There was nothing to tear out of the ground.

My rootlets drink the water of the marshes of the Loire-Atlantique but they don't keep me upright.

I don't know where my father was before. On what land and beneath what sun?

I am hydroponically grown. A boy born in a petri dish, made to float like the hyacinths on the ponds around our family home.

'Stay right here and grow. Don't ask too many questions that we can't answer.'

One day, I go to church with my grandfather. I don't know why, I guess we were at his house on a Sunday. I find myself entering a giant brand-new cone of composite rock and zinc tiles. It's a modern church, to his delight. After the hymns, I walk down the centre aisle not knowing where I'm going. When I reach the priest towering above me, I see his intrigued eyes land on me. I don't make the sign of the cross. I don't know how. I open my mouth like all the people ahead of me. My father always told me, 'Adapting and imitating others is the key to success.' The priest puts something on my tongue. It's flavourless.

When I get home, I tell my father, 'I took communion.'

He sits up on the beige leather couch where he takes his day-long Sunday nap, exhausted by his never-ending workweek. He stares at me and I sense an unexpected rage rising. I think that he couldn't predict that all-controlling madness either. He forbids me to go back. He doesn't curse my grandfather. Instead, he tells me, in the twisted logic of dual origins, not to let myself be unduly influenced by him.

Then he spits out, half-seated, eyes blazing, 'You're a Muslim.' Me: 'Okay.'

On a daily basis, my father tells me, with a look, in a threatening tone, to be completely discreet, to be like everyone else. At the same time, I have to follow his rules, and not become like everyone else.

My father doesn't drink. He's at the kiosk in front of the football stadium, but he's drinking coffee. I can smell it on his breath, which is different from the other fathers'. He goes home after the match, never to the bar. He keeps to himself but never expresses his contempt for the men in the village, or not to me. Which is important, huge, rather.

He saves his contempt for me. That's my lot.

Not once did he tell me that those people, those men, didn't deserve our efforts to integrate. But he knew. He knew that he would never win his place among them. At no moment did he belong. We will never belong.

And then, there's my mother.

My buffer of a mother, always calm, never violent. My white mother who keeps me close, my mother accused with looks or words of keeping me for herself, of preventing me from diving deeper into my roots, my origins, even as my cousins plunge in. My mother and her warm gurgling stomach on which I rest my sleepy head in the afternoons, my mother who's afraid for me as a child in the streets of Tangier, my mother who keeps me in living rooms full of women, who doesn't allow me to wander, my mother who's so beautiful it hurts. My mother with the pale eyes I don't have. My mother who blames herself for not having seen my otherness, my mother who cries and begs my forgiveness, tears in her green eyes, my mother who always knew why she wanted to protect me, and my erased mother, my mother who says yes, my mother who doesn't speak the same language as the others loudly sniggering , my gentle mother, too gentle, who irritates me, my gentle and tender mother, her tenderness that saves me from the paternal violence that erupts into our daily lives.

And then, the perpetual jousting between her and him.

From what I remember, we're in a restaurant, the one in the industrial estate, and I'm trying to think about something else. The ceilings are high but large awnings covered with the trattoria's logo darken the room. My father is bragging, showing off without imagining for one second that no one is actually listening to him.

He says to me, to wake everyone up, 'Did you see *Valeurs Actuelles* on Pépé's couch?'

My mother tenses, ashamed, but ready to defend herself and her family.

He says, 'Have you heard him talk about the benefits of colonialism?'

She's red with anger and I'm jubilant.

Pollock loin with *beurre blanc* and Neapolitan pizza.

In the middle of the large air-conditioned room, our round table and my father pretending to be on the right side.

But just yesterday, in a large house on the north side of town, between the tree-lined driveways and the forged iron gates, he made himself so small. We were on their turf and it was time to prove ourselves.

On the lawyer's wide patio, the adults were eating as evening fell, and I saw him smoke and drink. How my father changes, depending on the light, the looks, and the weather . . .

We were at their house, and the boys spoke formally to their parents. *S'il*-vous-*plaît*. Other than that, they were nice, all blond, already wearing ties at age eight. I thought: the men and their sons in this world are allowed to be gentle and handsome, not like in my world. The girls, an amorphous block of blouses and navy-blue pleated skirts, as I recall, harassed my sister the whole dinner. Their mouths heaping abuse from between pairs of golden or ginger braids. And my father pretending not to see, not to hear. The pebbles they gathered in the garden and threw at my sister, cackling like old ladies, already consumed by hate. And my father pretending not to see, not to hear their nasty remarks about her Nike TNs and her hair long enough to sit on.

And my father pretending not to see, not to hear.

Silence in the car going back to the countryside where it belongs, quietly leaving the city. The narrow streets widen and become straighter, soon wide asphalt and not a single cobblestone; a smooth, black road. Back on the periphery, on our way home, my sister crying in the passenger seat, me observing my father the defector who's staring straight ahead. I wonder what he can possibly be thinking.

Where's his guilt? Where's his pride? For me too, the shame that's come to swallow me whole.

Like with Samuel on the bus. Every morning in the dawn light, cold and fear weighing heavy in my stomach, I watch him arrive. At first, it's a relief, a joy, to see him standing beneath the bus shelter. The air is crisp and everyone huddles up to wait. He sits next to me, and, before the day that will be difficult to endure, there's a nice ride and his light hand on my shoulder. The other kids are yelling, they're loud, but the two of us, lying down almost, camouflaged by the tall seats, are protected.

It lasts a few weeks, maybe more. I can't remember. Samuel and the guilt that poisoned my brain for so long.

And one day, amid the barrage of insults and fighting words that secondary school kids toss at one another – dirty slut, scumbag, pauper, dirty Arab, sheepshagger, bastard, cocksucker, mong, loser – there's this: 'The two bus fags.'

I try to understand why this provokes such panicked fear inside me. A vibration that sends a warning to my slumbering secret, pulling at its roots, the water trembling around the house, the school, the whole town.

The next day, I didn't stand beside Samuel under the metallic shelter. He didn't react, huddled up like an animal that senses such things. We got on the bus and I decided not to take the risk. I was afraid of freeing the secret nestled in my gut so when he tried to sit next to me, I didn't budge, I didn't move up closer to the window to make room. I stayed where I was, motionless, staring into nothing, ignoring him, already starting to forget him.

Painful, electric tension between our two bodies. I finally get rid of him with: 'I'm not a fag! Keep going.'

He goes to the front of the bus and sits near the driver.

I never looked at him again. He understood my cruelty. I never sat beside him again.

This interlude was a call to order, and proof of my weakness back then, my capitulation to societal shame. Condolences to my dreams under the covers. The justified fear gnawing at my thoughts and chasing away my fantasies.

And then, the garden becomes less of a refuge. The countryside no longer sounds the same. Bulldozers and rivers of cement, meadows levelled and marshes drained.

I don't see the swarms of grasshoppers anymore. The ones that flew up with every step, tiny genies of the meadows, their stomachs apple-green.

I don't see the fat grey crickets anymore. The ones that opened their wings blue as turquoise along the gravel-lined path. Clumsy jinn.

The desire to leave forms in my mind as nature ceases to be a refuge. I stop wanting to climb trees and spend more of my time thinking about leaving, praying at night to be transported somewhere I'll no longer have to answer to my family for anything. I want to go somewhere the local boys on motorbikes can't ride to. That's my idea of a safe place. Somewhere, I'll understand later, they're not allowed to enter.

I think and I pray in glum housing lots, at night under orange lights, belly full of alcohol.

I think and I pray stretched out on bundles of hay, at night, under the stars, not listening to the other boys sloshing beer on themselves.

I think some more and I pray so hard on my bike, along the dirt paths that lead to houses full of cheap vodka, shouting and loud music that overflows into the fields of sweetcorn and rape.

I think so hard and I pray so hard that I make it happen. I leave home and my parents. I bury the forbidden orgasms and the fists in my mouth. I leave and I promise success and pride but all the same, I bring with me the desires that want to emerge at any cost.

It's with them that I learned the great power of denial, of invoked amnesia. I leave home and I forgive no one. I forget.

The Bonfire

My father didn't take my leaving well, of course. I sensed as much from my mother's voice over the phone, and the tears she didn't hold back. She told me he flew into a rage and lit a bonfire in the garden. She admitted, racked with guilt, that she hadn't been able to stop him from reading my childhood diaries, or the more recent ones, my diaries of desire. She cried because she hadn't been able to keep him from doing what he did. I don't say much. I imagine: fury in his eyes, a metal poker, all those pages with my words and scribbles tossed into the fire, the pages I wrote as a teenager and the ones I wrote last month.

The taunts, the anger, the drawings of penises, it all goes up in smoke, his fault, his hand. Flames licking at my memories committed to Leclerc notebooks, consuming sketches of my first lovers, whom I can't remember without those analytical, detailed outlines of their facial features and their dicks. A perfect catalogue, and now that it's gone they'll disappear behind closed doors. I'd left my classified notebooks sitting out, forgetting, I suppose, my father's appetite for things that are none of his business.

I'm sure you could see the black smoke of my blazing secrets over the empty A-road.

He discovers who I am and decides he won't stand for it.

He drinks whiskey and in despair performs his *salat* prayer.

I learn this from my mother and sister, their voices choked by sobs.

At first I tell my friends that I want to die, that the shame and fear will be the end of me, that I can't even breathe, but after a few days, I start to laugh at him. My ribcage loosens, twitching with grief, but it's laughter that comes out.

I laugh hysterically behind the wheel of my beaten-up white car, then I laugh in the metro, I laugh alone at home over vegetables browning in the pan.

I think: How weak! How tragic! The man's incapable of empathy . . . What a tiny little world he lives in . . . Terrified of sex and any and all bodily fluids . . . How cruel!

I'm sure you could see the black smoke of my blazing secrets rising above the tile roof.

Why not continue to avert his gaze?

Why not apply the method of silence that he taught me so well?
Why not maintain the status quo of my caged suffering?
Why liberate the memories I'd spent so long neutralising?

In Paris, I study. I couldn't tell you what, it doesn't matter. I let the days pass. Sometimes I turn in excellent work and other times, utter mediocrity. It depends on my level of anxiety.

When my parents manage to get me to pick up the phone, I tell them, 'Everything's fine. *Kolchi mzyan.*'
And that's about it. The *hshouma* lasts for years.

In the midst of this period, outbursts of belligerent anger.

It might start because I left my phone behind on a counter or maybe I can't find my keys. There needs to be a trigger, something that reveals to me my inability to focus. An element however miniscule that echoes in the silence.

Plus, I don't know, I have rage in my genes bubbling up. The feeling is sudden, it grabs me by the scruff of my neck and throws me into the abyss. I do whatever the anger tells me, an obedient underling. I shatter things in my apartment. A glass, a computer or a pen that I crush between my fingers, leaving them coated in blue ink.

Muddled thoughts.

And then I understand: obscenity and indecency are fleeting, but it's the knowledge that all my paper confessions have been burnt that leaves me speechless.

Learning that he burnt my most intimate thoughts to ash prompts a deep breath and immediately after, silence. So this is where his unquenchable thirst to control everything leads us.

I think this is when I start to forget anything and everything. My memory wavers, shock a gust of wind blowing away every thought.

Yes, this is when the thick fog settles in, my brain cells unable to retain a single thing.

I'm sure you could see the black smoke of my blazing secrets between the treetops.

I don't say much to my mother. 'It's fine, don't worry, it's not your fault . . .'

This is the beginning of the haze. I go months without seeing or calling them. I'm frozen, stunned, unable to think. Not one distinct idea emerges, my fears melt together.

Though, in any case, in my family, you don't leave. I take the train once or twice a year to visit them. They greet me with a forced smile, a pat on the shoulder.

The trip is the soft fabric of the train seats and a lump in my throat.

Once I reach the front steps of my parents' long cream-coloured house, I tremble. I'm ashamed.

I stare at the ground and I share nothing of my life.

My father doesn't spare me a glance. It's very cold, the white tiling on which I used to play feels hostile. My boyhood bedroom is bare.

A few warped photos from adolescence hung with blutack remain on the walls. There's still the gaping hole in the door, which reveals the broken composite panels hiding behind the white paint. It's in the shape of my father's foot. I don't sleep that night. I smoke at the patio door, looking at the sheer blackness of nature. Birds of prey screech, the sound echoes. I can't think. My secret is out in the open.

The house feels damp, as though damp has risen from the lake and mixed with the black smoke emitted by burning sheets of paper. It smells like embers and ash, and I don't want to go back inside. The fog enters my thoughts, continues to spread. The drizzle falling around the house gives off the scent of mud, but maybe it's just the nausea of knowing I've been unmasked.

I want to be somewhere else. I want to be home. But back in my studio-apartment perched at the top of my building, my head is still foggy.

Amid the Fog

It's been a few years now since I left and my father refused to accept it.

I might break into a million pieces, the danger omnipresent in my gut. Everything's black and I have no idea what tomorrow will bring. I'm nothing but images and grief. Fear has flattened me into pixels. I scroll in absence.

When the anxiety arrives, my body is on high alert, it feels as though even the most microscopic vessels in my body are dully vibrating at a particularly unbearable speed. I sense the familiar acidity spreading. Air is summoned into my lungs with great force but it's tedious work, and I'm tempted to smack my head with the palm of my hand to shake my neurons back into place. I'm in the metro or the street but really, I'm always in the same place when my sickness attacks: my memories.

I say anxiety, but it's actually my memory trembling and yielding, it liberates the past, all of it, inside my body. The sensations are from the years I spent at the back of the garden inhaling the smell of oak. This feeling was already clawing at me, part of my daily life, when I was seven, maybe eight. When it comes, I can't do anything but replay memories and latent fears in my mind.

Every time, I'm propelled into the 'before'. No images, total darkness, so it's my body that sees. It's my body now that is forced to endure the contrite childhood, consumed by fear. My body now that is compelled to live these memories over and over, through my stomach, my legs, my shoulders and my throat.

It's been a few years now since I left and my father refused to accept it. The fog is thick and I don't know where I am anymore. No, it's not easy to know where to go. Where to stand, what to say.

Within that damp haze, I feel enormous apprehension about life in its entirety, the network of water veins it forms, all those streams and tributaries, all those obscure crossings. I see all my friends succeed or fail but with intention, they have a plan. And what I'm trying to express here is that my intention, my plan, is unliveable. I know from the start that there's nowhere to drag my tired body but *there* – the place to which I resigned myself even as a little boy.

I shirk my responsibilities. I remain completely removed from reality. I can't make it my own. I don't know how to go about digging myself a tunnel, a little burrow just for me, through the beckoning world.

Routine, silence, I avoid other people for a long time. It's been a few years now since my father burnt everything.

In a silent room, I watch others push their bodies to the limit on grey and orange weight machines.

My body has to be impeccably presentable. It can't show that I don't know what I'm doing with my life. I feel nauseous. I think about their idiotic norms as I sip my chocolate protein shake. I wish I had big pecs like that small stocky queer in the corner. I wish I had a big booty like that girl jumping about by the window. I wish that my forehead was even smoother. I can already tell where the lines of old age will emerge. I realise the power of my upbringing. Be presentable, be well groomed and able to articulate.

Irreproachability is the primary consideration in my interactions with others, so much so that often I remain silent for fear of saying something stupid. I examine my body, pitiless. I see its weaknesses, its thinness, my angular face.

I'm still skinny, my ankles like two shrub stalks. Fragile. I wish I was anchored to the ground by solid muscular legs that supported a sturdy back and round shoulders. I'm at the mercy of this flat body.

In the centre of Paris, a pulsing machine where despair meets renewal, I climb the cogs, I find activities.

Often, I'll go outside to walk, walk, walk.

To feel an ache in the soles of my feet, focus on that. It only takes a few streets to quiet my brain and not be consumed by anxiety. Most importantly: don't think about my ferocious sexual desire. Compartmentalise it. Don't succumb to the easy, obvious relief.

And yet beast always beats brain in an overwhelming victory. Something explodes inside me, seeping into my bones. It spreads to my dick, which gets hard as I walk, rubbing against my wet and waiting skin. It's as if I'm making love to the street. I wish the feeling would slide off me but it sticks instead, it clumps in my memory and there's only one way for me to relax: walk about and enter other people's desires.

Fling myself against strangers' bodies, who said anything about pleasure, be enveloped in the heat of men I meet and make them come.

Absence, habit, I avoid anything that will make waves.

I hide out for months. When I look at people it's with an uncertainty that I try to mask, a matter of pride. The few friends I have talk around me. I say nothing. Everything is hazy.

I think: there's no refuge, none, nowhere, in any circumstance. No such thing as a calming look. I need a cave, a hole.

A break from all the 'You people.' From the 'Someone like *you.*'

But there's no refuge from smouldering men and frigid balls.
    What I mean is, they're on fire but I'm frozen.

I listen to people's stories and think that maybe I could steal them. Slide into their skins and live out my life in theirs. Often, on my walks, I see television sets in bars. I see scenes of football in saturated colours on screens suspended in a corner as men watch.

The players are oracles for some but I have no idea who they are. To me, they bring back smells of sweat and of ecstasy, and reveal the chasm between me and other men. In my past, they run across green grass on a big television in front of a group of their ever-adoring fans.

But I was looking at the sky so I didn't have to figure out the rules. I'm such a disaster on the pitch at the little stadium, every Saturday, three kilometres from our house, with the other neighbourhood boys, that my father gives up. I can still see myself crying on the way there and back. I invent an allergy to shin pads, so they slip cotton wool between my skin and the plastic.

Nowadays, my father says, 'Don't exaggerate . . . I never forced you to play football . . .'

It makes me melancholy that I find them worth admiring. Those men in synthetic shorts.

I continue my wandering, the same sharp jab in my groin leading me into bedrooms and towards bodies that I couldn't recognise today. I forget them one by one, a sieve under my brain.

And then go home, on the bed staring at the ceiling, depressed, not wanting them to ever touch you again with their dry fingers and slick tongues. Heaving sobs, the kind of shame you never get used to. I get up, go for my daily walk around the city but the mist is still so thick. After walking my sadness for hours, I wish I could conk out. Eyes prickling, muscles stabbing, jaws clenched, but no sleep.

It's those images in my head. Flames consuming my words and revealing my secrets to my father.

One day, I assert, 'White people don't understand the blood imperative . . .'
　　Someone tells me I'm wrong. Rightly so.

Another day, I say, 'The French don't understand our biological loyalty . . .'
　　Someone comments, 'You talk about your family a lot.'

I don't know how to do otherwise.
　　I don't think that the ideal of total autonomy, in other words a voluntary uprooting, could ever be in my future. And yet, I feel much less anxiety when I'm here in the city, far from them, as compared to in my family home.

Despite all my anger at their silence, something remains of what was instilled in me as a child. I know how to stay in line.

I'm terrified of not fitting into people's little (locked) boxes, so when I enter a universe in which I can't possibly mention everything that's made me who I am, I don't want to talk about my life. I say nothing personal. I always feel wholly inadequate, always a surprise. I can't find my place. I look but it doesn't exist. People don't make room for me. And I hear terrible things, horrible things about Arabs.

I'm filled with every shade of rage but the colossus of my up-bringing always squashes it, the silence deafening.

I know how to stay in line, I got it from them.

I try to shake off my lethargy. I go for walks along the canal, or buy some pretty bracelets. These activities, I tell myself, were introduced into our daily lives as receptacles into which we can pour our troubles. They absorb my madness, my outings, though my thoughts still periodically slip into darkness.

The rural districts of Texas will remain Republican. French forests will undergo clearfelling.

The violence of men and the numbering of cypresses. Arabic won't be taught in schools.

The radio provides these pieces of information, which echo through the room. Such a long Monday.

I'm reminded of something someone says to me one day: 'I wanted to learn Arabic so I could defend myself in the streets.'

His words still thunder in my head. A handsome guy with eyes a light shade of green, whom I like a lot. Then he admits, 'I'm afraid of you.' I reject any similarity, any attempt to make us the same. In that same tough speak, he confides, 'You Arabs are either dangerous or you're faggots.'

But I don't feel quite like a faggot. I don't feel quite dangerous either. What I feel is the impulse to smash his head into the pavement when he says those tainted words with a sigh. He whispers it like we're confidantes, both initiated into that true truth.

It happens often. This sensing their desires projected onto me as if I'm supposed to dominate them or speak to them in a language I can't speak, as if that was my role.

Men search me for sexual power, for the pain of exile. They search, they scrutinise, they desperately sniff for the savage, the propensity for drama, the police that hate me, or the gob of spit on the ground, or that piece of Arab trash who comes to your house in the middle of the night to make you come.

One of my friends says to me, 'It's kind of hot . . . the colonist gaze on us. It's a way of assuming power.'

I don't take any joy from it. I'm tired. They watch and wait for the violence they assume is intrinsic to my being. They say, 'And your dad? Your mum? Do they still love you?'

They're disappointed to find out I'm not completely Arab either, that I'm mixed, diluted, less exciting. They look, they scrutinise, it's exhausting.

And often I say nothing.

Minding my manners, that way I have of 'always being nice', as my mother puts it. She's right to remind me that it's not about being good, or true, or cheerful. It's a personality defect. And so I'm compelled to smile, the same smile my father gives the racist old lady in the posh furniture store. The exact same reassuring smile that says 'I'm not dangerous, I'm a faggot,' or 'I won't steal anything, I'm rich.'

This lady forces a smile back. She seems tougher than the others. Usually the fear vanishes immediately, the furrowed brows relax, and a normal conversation ensues. I'm saccharine-sweet to her even though, like my father I'm sure, I'm filled with extremely violent urges. Preposterous fantasies that rise from deep in my body. We leave. We won't buy anything here, and my father stops talking.

And the time the green-eyed boy tells me, 'I wanted to learn Arabic so I could defend myself in the street'? Same thing. I'm very nice, remain very gentle. I'm sure that tons of people like me, pushed to the margins, condemned to a contagious otherness, will understand: play the game, show you belong.

I smile, cajoling, those extreme manners again, and as reserved as a nun. I open up the app and a stranger's written to me: 'You're North African . . . How does it make you feel to know that your entire community wishes it could kill you?'

Grindr is, in essence, the gateway to the hell of the future. A reminder of sorts, tick tock, the big bad monster will come out soon and destroy our worlds, sever attachments, squash peace and harmony. We'll be sent back to a place I'm not sure I even come from. France is home to a raging beast slumbering beneath the surface. Best not to provoke it.

Amid the fog, my lovers' faces. They only ever emerge in my dreams. On occasion, when I hear a street name, I'll think: I visited a stranger's bedroom there. The city opens its gaping mouth, all I have to do is nestle inside.

I feel like puking when they write to me: 'I'm looking for young Arab meat.'

The ones who bite their tongues end up asking my name, they don't always know it. I admit, sometimes I make one up. I'll tell them 'Paul'. Or maybe 'Clément'. I see their eyes cloud over, confusion. So then, I'm doing the same thing, looking for what they expect from me. I try to guess what they want me to give them in the dark, in the hollow of their necks.

Most often, it's savageness. Most often, the Arab is what they're after.

My body gets used to it. This intimacy with others is the only way it can handle the fear and the shame. It's so easy to forget yourself, all those cavities. I burrow into them as often as I can.

This helps me fall asleep, instead of roaming the city or lying on the hardwood floor, static in my brain.

This helps me calm my heart endlessly beating louder and louder in a painful rhythm, instead of staying home alone and going round in circles.

I don't spare much thought to the few boys who like me. I barely grant them a weekly slot. Some try to take me out to dinner, others want to walk around hand in hand. I play the game. I tell myself: I do what I have to. Sometimes I glean mild satisfaction from it. The glances at our bodies close together on the metro or the street make me almost cheerful. I tell myself: It's fine, I'm a nice guy. But soon enough, I invent reasons to disappear. I raise my eyebrows, suddenly surprised at how attached they've become. I promise I didn't realise, not for a second, the feelings burgeoning in front of me.

It's only now.

Only now that I discover their pain.

I think about T., his expensive haircut, his Algeria shirt, and the loafers he wore with Adidas joggers. That's what seduced me. Plus the circles under his eyes, his brown, hairy stomach. We met at a party. He looked at me, he said 'Evening.' I found it pretentious. But we talked a little and all of a sudden he went, 'Oh, I see. You're the kind of faggot who does Ramadan. You want to wash away your sins.'

That struck me as funny, I think. And then something developed, in spite of myself. We saw each other regularly, at a rhythm obviously forced on me. I remember how angry he would get when I didn't show up for a date.

He would lash out, 'Seriously, who raised you? Who gave you the right to treat other people like this?'

He would call me, full of what I thought was too much speed or 3-MMC (but which had to have been mainly sadness), and say, 'You'll see. No one but me will put up with your little disappearing acts . . . You won't find better than me . . .'

I remember my indifference when he had his meltdowns. No one gave me the right to disappear, I claim it. He wishes I would remember the stories he told me, wishes I felt like sleeping with him for several nights in a row. It doesn't even occur to me. Eventually T. will lose his mind. One night he'll send me a message meant to provoke, which I consider justified, now, when I think about it. But in the moment, I didn't understand. He broke up with me on the spot, we never saw each other again, not even by chance. For the best.

After that, an even greater void. There are moments when my boredom is so all-consuming . . . I don't know how to get past it.

One morning, I watched a video posted by an animal rights group on my phone. I didn't become a vegetarian. But there was something in the blood wildly spurting from the body of a slaughtered cow that caught my attention, something easy. My days are dark. And overlaying my daily thoughts, like a filter, was the image of my body resting underground amid the roots and insect tunnels.

I don't see a way out of the unhappiness lodged in my chest.

I wish I could shut myself away in the company of trees and light. But winter won't allow it. Along the Seine, there are only the skeletons of plane trees. The cobblestones are dangerous

and people walk heads bowed to avoid sticky droplets. I spend
these dark months in latency.

One day E. knocks at my door. Surprise visit.

'Bit late to be sleeping.'
        'I don't know what else to do.'
        'Have you thought about talking to someone?'

Two weeks later, I've fallen into the trap.

In the room, there's a couch with bright orange and purple up-
holstery. Sequined pillows with tiny shimmering insets. Directly
above, a crayon drawing in a light wood frame. The other walls
are bare. On the right, a wicker armchair and a lady with short,
ash-coloured hair staring at me. I start talking very quietly. She's
forced to lean forward, to ask me to repeat myself, patiently. I
think: this is her job after all, to listen attentively. And then, I
develop a taste for it. I tell her things that I've never thought
about before. She's the receptacle for my ideas. If I leave them
here in her office, I don't have to act on them. I lie at first. Then,
amid my inventions, things are revealed. Truths emerge, I confess, they explode in front of me. I develop a taste for it. I go
every week, enthused by our sessions.

One morning, she smiles with that half-amused, half-worried
look of hers, behind her kooky glasses, as she listens to me.
She allows the silence to linger at the end of the session, which
is unusual.

Finally, she whispers, 'You need to break away from your
culture.'
        I freeze, all the trust I'd let myself put in her shattered.
        'Say again?'
        'You need to leave behind your culture and all its rules.'

I don't say another word. In a split-second, it's as if I had been an animal observed in a cage since birth and I hadn't noticed this pair of human eyes of me. I'm a wild beast behind bars. She saw everything I told her through the prism of *my culture*. I know exactly what that means.

I stand up to pay and by flipping the end-of-session ritual, she understands the spell has been broken and stares at me in surprise. I didn't come here to be given another injunction.

I ignore her calls for a few weeks. She eventually gives up.

It's not pretty after that, my life still a mess, everything muddled. To be honest, I can't imagine myself being brave enough to end it. Though I thought about it, usually in the morning: what if I did it today? Just end it all.

Yes, there are images of slaughterhouses and other things, too, balconies where I go to smoke a cig, motorways and the onrush of cars that could break me in half. I think about the end, how I could do it.

Why not jump once and for all into the void?

I truly can't see a future for myself. What destiny? In any case, I don't care, I keep on making a little money smiling at faceless customers from behind a counter.

I dream of the end. Voices echo in my head, forecasting my death in varied circumstances. I don't spare them much thought, they're just the backdrop. A filter over the rage and anger.

And in the end, I don't do it. I fuck a little, I go out, melt into the night, into the club music pounding against the breeze-block walls. Though I don't find much comfort there. I like to dance and then forget, watch a few queers duelling it out, I find the whole thing entertaining. You shouldn't think I never smiled during those years. There was fun, the occasional fit of laughter.

I rely on a tool that I've had for as long as my faulty memory can remember: I talk to myself. Though I don't argue. The point is not to comment on my inner emotions.

I talk aloud, and loudly, in my apartment. If I have to meet up with someone, I imagine the conversation to the slightest detail, I prepare my facial expressions, my witty remarks. When I get home, I replay the scene. I go through the misunderstandings and I solve them. Of course I imagine myself, if I'd had the courage to act differently, more interesting.

I talk all day long, nonstop. I don't mean I'm thinking aloud, it's something different. I'm writing. I write alone in the silence of my bedroom or the elevator. The sentences I conjure into the air disappear automatically.

In reality, I'm searching for meaning. Some beauty to my despair. I try to express this out loud. Sometimes it's too much, the voice takes over. I converse more with myself than I do with others, shut inside for weeks without seeing a soul.

So, my daily life, after the bonfire a few months earlier: coffee and a tiny pill to shut up the voice. Wandering, pretending to work, pretending to study.

Insomnia, ceiling above the bed where my pain and then my apathy take shape in the form of missed opportunities.

Terrible shyness, my voice never loud enough to assert anything whatsoever. Lily flowers, dirty windowpanes and CBD. It doesn't work.

A green night in the dark of winter, I ring a doorbell and a man opens, shirt unbuttoned. This one's a philosophy professor, but it could be anybody. My dick planted between his open legs and the boredom eases.

Generally speaking, though, everything's hazy. Voice, silence, voice, silence.

There's the little pill the GP thought would be a good idea. Occasionally, I'll take a second one, sometimes more. They calm me down, help me pass the time in the middle of the fog. All that damp opaqueness is far from reassuring.

My apartment reeks of orange pistils, the smell overpowering, I can't think straight anymore. All the better. Winter drags on and then comes to a close.

The nice weather slowly settles in. I return to the old house for a bit but it's another failure. Very quickly, to my dismay, August arrives. No crescendo, no nothing. My life is tremendously boring. I'd be scared if it was otherwise. I do everything in my power to ensure it's not.

I nap in the garden, staying out of my father's way. I don't text any of my former friends who live nearby. I stay in the sun, indecisive, nauseous.

Shimmering sadness.

What I mean is: under the synthetic mosquito net my entire body is dripping as the cruel morning sun, already so powerful, beats down and I'm damp all over. I glisten.

It's 300 degrees and I see (from the tree tops to the blue cream of the swimming pool) a sparrow fall. It glides onto the oily flat surface and drinks, beak gaping: it laps up the chlorinated water.

I start listening to voices on YouTube that speak of sacred things, and in the few animals that remain in this changing suburb, I see angels and jinn. Like when I was little, I try to rediscover the magic of the forests but not a single ghost wants to talk to me.

So August was very gloomy. Without heat, for me, or rather heat like a brick oven, and my clay body scorched at the end. But August, without question, didn't amplify anything, didn't liberate anything.

I have a memory of another bird; this one crashes into my windscreen one morning.

And I don't make a sound, my entire body as dense and heavy as a pile of rope.

I think back to the two-headed birds with human faces that populated my dreams when I was a little boy. Stories about biodiversity at Chernobyl and my child brain inventing the gentlest of monsters.

The white car that accompanies me through fields and towns. A change from the metro, I can sing as loud as I want and visit the sea. But soon enough, I want to go back to the city. I'm suffocating.

The fog is always thicker around the family house. My father ignores me. The occasional glance at my long hair, dark curls down to my neck, the jewellery on my fingers and wrists.

He asks me, 'Where are you trying to belong by wearing that stuff? Who are you trying to look like with your hair like that?'

One day, on the train to visit my parents, the driver hit a roe deer.

The carriage is still, tilting slightly into the void. I see the countryside through the window, groves, a sparrowhawk perched on a fence. I contemplate the motionless fields, which no one crosses, except maybe a guy on a tractor come to sprinkle the rape with toxic products. Suddenly, there's a terrible odour. Not of pesticides, it's muckspreading. A foul stench gradually fills the train blocked on the tracks. It smells like shit. The providential wait turns into a nightmare in air tainted by manure a farmer must have spread close by.

It's unbearable. My body already tense with disgust, I feel the first tremor of anxiety. I tell myself: there's no way we're going to stay here all day, stuck because of a dead deer, we'll suffocate. I see children moving down the aisles. They grimace, make funny faces that provoke a certain feeling in the base of my spine. They shout, shake the seats. I sense a familiar pressure inside my head, the one that crushes my neurons. Suddenly I don't feel very good. And then sweat running down my back, a burst of heat, trapped in this SNCF seat. I decide to get up, grab some air. Buzzing and flashes of blue, the train seats spinning.

I find myself passed out in the corridor, alone.

A boy opens the door, there's that weird pressure noise. He's staring at me. It's embarrassing. He says, 'You want me to lift your legs? You're really pale.'

I nod, still lying on the ground. He grabs my shins and holds my legs against his lower stomach. Blood circulates. I feel better.

Once I've recovered, I feel like crying from the humiliation. I wish I could get off at Angers and go back to Paris. I tell him, 'Thank you.' Then I stand up.

The train gets moving again right after. I can't remember if it still stunk or not. I don't want to go home. Visits to my parents' house feel like endless and impossible returns.

Landscape full of bulldozers, the clouds of sparrows have disappeared, the electrical wires are bare. The carriage crosses the landscape of my memory, my how things have changed. And not in the right direction.

My mother tells me that the deer have stopped crossing the garden at dawn.

I can't tell her about the city. The way it triggers the slow collapse of all my landmarks and always that same haze in my mind, my penis guiding my legs as if I was a dumb animal, plus the void, the silence, the fear of doing something with my life.

Every time I go back, I tell myself: I forget these houses too quickly. These supermarkets. These football stadiums.

I realise that I'm forgetting something else, the country in the background. The one buried in my chest, that's not truly mine. Morocco violently comes back to me.

I'm left speechless. All I want is to smell the tarmac, smell the petrol on the corniche.

I miss it.

Some part of my diluted self is abruptly jolted and says to me: What are you going to do with your roots across the Mediterranean? Have you even thought about it? Will you be buried there? Are you rejecting your ancestors? Where exactly do you think that'll get you? Whiteness or bust, is that it? You gonna keep watering yourself down for long?

Some part of me screams inside my head: Don't dilute yourself any more than you already have . . . Don't water yourself down more than you already have been . . . Where's the Arab in you? You're not taking care of it . . . Don't dilute yourself more than you already have . . .

I have dinner with a friend and she talks about her grandparents.

I say nothing. I think about stolen land and the tortured bodies of the people whose land was stolen. I listen as she tells me about the humiliation and subjugation her grandparents felt when those appropriated spaces were taken back. I rack my brain for how to listen to her talk about her family of colonists expelled from Algeria. I surprise myself by feeling empathy for them. I don't know what I'm supposed to feel.

I don't think that my grandfather or grandmother ever told me about their anger or their indignation. I truly don't know what I'm supposed to feel. I heard, plenty of times, about the bodies blanketing the roads during the war, my grandmother saw them. Arab bodies on the ground, lined up along the paths. I don't know how I inherited that anger. No one told me much of anything. No one taught me to hate the colonisers. Ferocity swells in me when my friend tells me about her poor ancestors from northern France who migrated to find happiness. They didn't get swallowed by the waters. No, they were allowed to pass.

Strangely enough, I blame the sea, which engulfs the men and women who cross it today.

I wish I was someone else's creature, that that someone would decide my fate, the sun would explode, turn red and die on the earth's surface spilling forth its lava and I would melt into the universe, completely forgotten and without a world to save or abandon.

It's always been that way. I never knew where to go, what to say, what to do.

I'm at my grandmother's, she's singing, something that matters rising from deep in her throat in the language I don't know. A song of lament, of faith. She squeezes my hand with her warm palm. I hate this moment. It tears me up inside not to be able to understand her. I remain silent and look at the ground, ashamed. She laughs as she hugs me, 'It's not a big deal.'

Sure, not a big deal for the one giving. But for the one receiving, there's so much left to be done with those words. The work of a century. Decode a message I've already forgotten.

I'm exhausted, is what I'm mainly trying to say. Compared to everyone else, I don't have the energy to do anything and I don't understand why. Often I can't even move. Then it becomes clear to me that I won't ever do anything to make my father proud.

She rises and comes back with scalding tea and *sfenjs*. The smell of the beignets is strong and I'm a little dazed by my nap. I'm tempted to tell her about my memories. To describe the violence with words in a shared language, words that would push away the silence, push back the lethargy. But I'm incapable of expressing complex thoughts. I can only talk about lunch or isn't the sky blue today. My lack of vocabulary is a plaster cast, and I'm paralysed inside. Even though I know that here, in my grandmother's person, is a place my flawed memory could express itself. A place of silent reflection that will be taken away because I lack the codes. She lives here, and I can't decipher her language.

For a long time, I could see hardly anything through the alien trees that made up my world. A dense landscape in which the miracle of exile inevitably, and exclusively, drew my gaze.

My father, whom 'family reunification' tore away from the fig trees and the mountain that kept them starving, left a trail of breadcrumbs in me. Though I can't understand why I'm the chosen heir to the story. It doesn't make sense. In a burst of enthusiasm, he starts telling me about eating orange peels, about his mouth chomping down, chewing, swallowing. He transports me to another land but it's opaque to me. I can make out branches, I glimpse his grandmother's face, I've seen her portrait at my grandmother's house. He tries to teach me about hunger, about his sleeping face on beaten earth. I think I'm listening but at the same time, it's impossible to follow. As a child, I'm meant to understand the miracle of exile and the totality of misery. He mocks me, angry almost that I live in the comfort that he's provided for me. I sense in my father's voice mild disdain for my demands and frivolities. And one rule: always view the abandoned land as somewhere you leave, and never somewhere you go back to. In my mind, I construct Morocco as one of those places you need to flee; returning would be nonsensical, idiotic. With his descriptions that distance his country, my father feeds me a picture-postcard world. But even as he tells me there was no choice but to leave, he misses it. His story blends the ideal country and hunger, a cruel and perfect world.

It didn't make sense to me yet. Pain as hybrid.

Imagine living surrounded by fields, by the wetlands of the Atlantic shore, and coming from the Beni-Snassen Mountains.

I'm still looking for something.

In Paris, the smell of parks at night. I don't know if the men I encounter want my desire, my death, or whatever's in my pockets. I see the heads of monsters in the hollows of their faces.

But what I want is moss and leaves.
Brown leaves that rot and stir up memories in the air.
The dampness of the trees clings to the darkness, a vague tugging at what's left of my memory and the mystery of my existence.
Large black craters appear in the sky of leaves but you can't see the stars.
Classic Paris.

How to leave the world?
How to not hear them anymore, not see them anymore?

How to get rid of the screens that virtualise my thoughts?
Disconnect from the commands inside my head and while I'm at it, the putrid streams of information in which overly muscular men and unrepentant fascists roll together in the mud?

How to leave the world?

How to forgive and organise your life and advance towards the sun?

How to leave the world?

I walk within the fog and I wish it would clear.

The Death of Jeddi

Thursday, 14 January 2021. A text: 'He's close. Get here by tonight.'

Across France, an entire family mobilises, by train, by plane, by car, all the way to the bedroom that fills with our trembling, sweating, crying bodies, masks donned. It's very hot and I kiss his cheeks the way I'd imagined. I dare to grab his hand, because now I can. It's at the very end that modesty becomes irrelevant. It's ten p.m. and in the dark corridor my aunt explains, 'He hasn't eaten or drunk anything for two days now, and he hardly ever opens his eyes.'

I nod, I understand.

She adds, 'He's leaving us. He's decided.'

I hear the sound that alerts everyone to what's happening, that prepares us for the departing. I'd have thought that people always go quiet at the moment of their deaths, and then slip away into the silence. Not at all. Loud, rhythmic breathing echoes in the room. The 'death rattle', says my aunt. His breath stops momentarily, prompting necks to crane towards his face illuminated by the bedside lamp on his left, but always resumes. Against that laboured breathing, voices recite the Quran. Sobs mix with crisply articulated sacred words. By this point, I've already completely forgotten the trip, the time the train arrived or even reaching the house. And before that, the city where I live and my daily routine. I can't remember a single lover. Everything – the young men and their desires and the silence of my apartment – has already sunk into the black void of denial.

What I mean to say is that the haze holding me captive is all encompassing.

Yet from that disarray emerges a home hospital bed on which my grandfather has been laid. Around 4:40 a.m., my body gives out, and lying on a pink and blue floral *7aifa* I doze off. I tell myself that if I sleep, he'll live a little while longer. I dream of angels. They gather around me, hissing and yowling in their terrible language, which sounds like rocks being ground to dust. There are three or four of them, endlessly circling to warn me, but I have no way to understand them.

The angels are unintelligible, just like the voices I hear from the kitchen. The family members who can't enter the bedroom or squeeze into the corridor to watch over him. There's too many of us, we have to alternate. We have to take turns. I think: Is this dying body the source of all our bodies? All our bodies in existence here and now as his reaches its end? I sleep at the foot of the *sedari* on which one of my cousins is lying. In her stomach floats a foetus waiting to be born.

A great-grandson who emerges from the void as my grandfather enters it.

Friday, 15 January 2021. My sister wakes me. 'Come. Please.'

Springing into the doorway, I hear his last breath. After that, things get hazy. I leave the bedroom and there's a very litany, at first just one voice: *La ilaha illa Allah.* There is no God but Allah. We'll collectively chant these words aloud but each in our own madness. I see my cousin lying on the floor, pale. I see M. throw up as I stroke his back. I walk through the house, shaky on my feet. I see faces stricken with grief, people don't know where they are anymore. I see my mother who squeezes my shoulders hard while I beat my head with my fists. I scream, 'It hurts.' I think she calms me down as if I were a small child. And then the sun rises and I don't know what we do. I help my uncle wrap a white scarf around his head. He smiles and I can't believe it. Like a scene out of a film. The windows need to be opened and the heat turned off. At one point, I vomit too. I touch him again and again. We divvy up spots around the bed to hold his hand that someone has slipped under the blanket, to keep his body warm a little longer. Everyone has their time to cry. I hear voices telling the women not to make too much noise, not to mourn so loudly, that tradition doesn't allow it. But their crying makes me feel better. If they cry, then I don't have to make any noise. They weep for me. He was the cornerstone. Now, the hustle to rebuild. Like little ants, they scatter to contact the mosque, the funeral home, and I don't know who else.

And then the loud swarms of visitors, a cup of burning-hot tea on my thigh, I don't hear a word anyone says to me. The neighbours offering condolences, I think. Men and women who are part of my extended family but I don't recognise them. I don't know if it's due to the unusual circumstances or my shaky memory. I forget everything and it's not from a lack of interest. I forget the sex of the unborn child, find it impossible to remember birthdays. I'll probably even forget the date of his death. I can't remember anything and it's not because I can't be bothered. I can remember very clearly the words said to me when I was five. I'll never forget the smell of that bedroom and his supple skin covered with liver spots that I was allowed to touch. My memory is a desert and beneath the sand lie waterholes, a deep thirst to remember things, except it's not always possible. When I said that it hurt, I meant in my arms and my legs and beneath my heart, the heat of something ripping away. And then, with his absence, the veil covering everything vanished. I can sense it already, on the threshold of grief – new clarity.

It's as if someone abruptly slashed the artery linking us to his world and his land. Blood spurts everywhere and I want to come running with buckets, yelling at the others to help me sponge up the deluge of words in a language I can barely understand. All the names from his past, all the forbidden stories and the secrets that concern us whether we like it or not. The lifeblood of our collective memory is disappearing, it's turning into quicksand, like inside my brain where I can't find my balance.

Though he was already archaic, to tell the truth, even before he left this world. His pearl-grey *gandura*, his cream *shashiya*, his silence, and then, out of nowhere, his thundering words. His blue-inflected gaze, the lump in his throat because he could sense my otherness. The immense respect he commanded, the impossibility of anyone standing up to him, his tragic, turbulent nights spent battling ghosts he hoped we would never see. Prison, his unfinished tattoos, his exile. Nothing that went unsaid in his lifetime can be dug up now. Everyone appears to be making their peace with it, except me and a few of his grandchildren. We smoke outside telling each other things-he-told-us-one-time-and-that-no-one-else-ever-knew.

The group investigation doesn't last. It's morning and I don't know what we do. I'm holding his hand gone cold. I hold it, they come, they lift him. He's heavy. I take refuge with the women. I can't bear to watch, can't bear to look at him.

Next, the burning affection of my family will nuke my brain. I don't remember anything of the days between my grandfather's passing and what follows. I return to Paris. That's the only reliable information I have, since I find it in my online calendar as I write this. In the interim, he was put into an oak box. I take a flight to Tangiers at the beginning of the following week. We land on the tarmac late that night. The moon is bright and people are debating its position. There's a long wait at customs. This time, no one asks me for my ID card, the green card I don't have. The agents look at us with pity in their eyes and as a unit we pass through the gates to the country. The apartment is overcrowded. We sleep where we can, on the floor, on makeshift beds in the kitchen. I slip out to the rooftop with my cousins, all ages combined. We light cigarettes and exhale smoke in the direction of the wind so the adults don't smell it. We eat sunflower seeds and listen to the muezzins. The city glitters but the usual sounds are absent, have been since an eight p.m. curfew was established, so it feels like a great collective mourning. We're entranced by a concert of stray dogs howling and fighting. His body travelled in the hold of an aeroplane to return to the land of origin. My aunt tells me she saw it out of the plane window. The luggage trolley is what really hit her hard, she adds, weeping. I don't know what to say. I gently console her, I wait for her to tire of crying into my shoulder. I'm ill at ease. All night long, the rooms fill with people who cry and people who comfort. I don't belong to either category. The next day, the women put on veils. I perform my ablutions, a huge knot in my stomach. Suddenly, one of my cousins shouts with joy. I hear her chair scrape across the floor tiles. I go to the rooftop. In the sky, a dance, a performance so beautiful you'd be hard-pressed not to admit God's existence. Birds, hundreds of thousands of tiny black sparkles, form moving clouds. Their backdrop the setting sun, they sculpt images for old and young alike. We go to pray in a modest mosque a short walk from his former house, in the small outlying neighbourhood that's now a banlieue. The house is surrounded by cement whereas, in every old photo that I've seen, it's clinging to a bare hill. My family before I was born, in flared trousers and turquoise-blue dresses that show the women's knees. I tell myself: Everything's changed, it's not like that anymore. The mosque walls are painted green and my father doesn't know how to pray. I give him my rug and tell him to follow my lead. I hear him sob during the *salat al-janazah*. My grandfather's coffin is carried to the ambulance, which is yellow and orange, and that's where a crowd of men shake my hand. I've never seen them before but they know who he was and who I am. But me, no idea, no hints, so many faces. They're come to seek a blessing, to wish me a place in paradise for you. I don't understand so I smile. I don't know where to put myself. We walk to the cars. I've lost my rug. The procession of cars reaches the hilly cemetery. I see bodies in white sheets, carried on simple stretchers. They're set on the ground and that's it. It's custom, I'd forgotten. This way, the ground can begin to devour them as soon as the ceremony ends. The idea fascinates me. The troop of vehicles reaches the muddy car park and everyone gets out, heads bowed. Only men. We reach the top of the hill. A hole has already been dug. I no longer have the strength to carry his coffin so men I don't know take over. They speak loudly, it's a matter of technique and co-ordination, can't go toppling the body. My trainers sink into the light brown earth, they stick when I try to change position. Every time I move, my feet get even heavier, inviting mud into and around my socks. The men suddenly grab shovels and pickaxes, and, praying out loud, they fill in the hole. I help with my hands, I don't know all the prayers. Suddenly, my father throws himself on the ground and turns into a burrowing animal. Someone stands him up, they tell him to calm down. Which strikes me as inappropriate. It's our dearly departed, not theirs. My father tells me to grab a shovel. I try, but the soil is so sticky, and the others are so fast, I'm slowing down the burial.

Once a mound of dirt covers the grave, figures approach. Exiles and women of the mountain. Their faces are wrinkled, regardless of age, even the little girls. Living in a place of death must have that effect. They live in shacks down below. They bring cut plants and flowers to the mourners in exchange for money. I take the leaves and, like everyone else, stick them in the ground. I see humus, I see mud, I see stems that squeal as they sink into the mix. It's a goodbye, it's the fog clearing. I can't even remember when it started. Summer. I see images of smoke and flames, I see my little notebooks destroyed and my deepest secret revealed.

Once the mound of flowered earth is complete, once we return to the car park and join the women, some of whom are enraged to have been pushed aside, chained to tradition, and others resigned amid their grief, I sense that a burden has lifted. That the shadows in my head are not as thick.

Suddenly, I can return to the apartment on Rue Mahatma Gandhi. I remember the names of avenues and squares. My memories creep back as I watch the city from the *sta7*. I spot the neighbourhood with the cinémathèque and the one with the Bara souk. I see the road that goes to Achakar.

Air steward, nice smile, Orly, moribund metro, it's on the way back that my memory returns. I recognise faces, identify lovers' streets, I remember friendships, and think how nice it would be to enjoy the beaming sun on a terrace. The cold wind burns my cheeks, and the morning light dries my droplets of tears. I feel liberated and I feel ashamed. It's as if I've found something, in the depths of my grief.

An Open Fruit

Back in Bariz, that something blooms and grows, nurtured by my restored memory. Restored by grief, I can finally make out what my future holds, and what a surprise.

I feel for my father, for his voice that breaks when he tries to pass as the head of the family sitting cross-legged on the *sedari*. He doesn't know the funerary customs and I tell myself that it's not his fault he taught me nothing.

Through my morning tears: dye my hair black and braid it, love all the people Allah has given me, and wear silver bracelets.

I unroll my rug on my bedroom floor and alone, I relearn the movements of prayer. Eyes shut, forehead and nose to the ground, a giving-in that cleanses and comforts.

Entire nights spent reciting the correct words to speak to God. I expect nothing. I enjoy watching my anxiety surrender.

I turn to YouTube to rediscover the sacred, emancipated from my conceited uncles and crowds of believers.

Nothing lasts, this too shall pass.

The slightest desire rising from the labyrinths of my mind comes as a relief, an object of fascination. Calm outside, turbulence inside.

Write lewd notes on my phone. Take a (female) lover, listen to Al Jazeera, and sleep . . . Walk, always, and drink Clairette.

I think about the totality of Allah and the future is like an open fruit. How odd after such a long period of suffering. My desires emerge from the burnt-down forest in a gush, a glimmer. I'm not trampling underfoot anymore. Now, I'm strolling.

Everything feels less frightening, more accessible. I start spending time with F., enjoying her company. We walk along the quays at night. We hold hands in the street. I kiss her breasts in her bedroom. On her furniture, accumulated objects, dusty flowers, skeletons. Her female body sparks a vague, calm longing. The fling only lasts a few days, but I like walking with her in the street, holding her hand. We talk about love and jealousy. She tells me she can't stand men who don't know how to share.

I don't respond. I'm not heterosexual enough to be petty.

I met F. by sleeping with her best friend. Then he left for Japan and it was just the two of us. She suggested we stroll along the quays. I said okay. Then she invited me to her place. Again, I said okay.

I remember tenderly touching the base of her neck with the tip of my index finger, when she has her back to me in the crowded metro.

F. and I discuss our brown skin. She's lived all over the world and doesn't really notice France's hostility towards her. She's since moved to her island, Majorca, with a handsome forty-year-old boyfriend. It's good she left.

I sense myself gradually getting better. Healed by colonial rage and the violence of grief. And with a greater understanding of my father. I tell myself: Finding who I am should no longer be the centre of my life.

Instead, I put olive and jojoba oil in my hair. I spend hours combing it, black with henna, shiny and soft. I braid my hair, and when I embrace F., her frizzy locks blend into my curls.

The bonfire took so much of me that I have no idea what remains. The guilt of reinventing myself, and the privilege too. The depression that comes to an end on its own and leaves me without a key to open the new door before me. Yes, that's exactly it — a vast fertile desert.

I know how to lie and burn bridges, clearly. Isolate parts of my history and keep them quiet. Don't let anyone know about them, the better to form a new mirage. I know how to do that, clearly, but as for the rest, I have no idea. Live outside of my memories? No idea. Move forward with intention and desire? It's the first time. I need a plan for my life, everyone else has one. A two-year plan at least. I have nothing for the moment, but I start to imagine, in this mare's nest of boredom, a path. I have wants, finally. Time to applaud them. I have things to say.

Walk around with this thought in my mind: bam bam bam. Like when you spot the cops, their faces lifeless, so proud of their truncheons. Feel like breaking things and using the wreckage to write my name and the names of people like me.

Feel like telling them in a booming voice: 'FYI we're on our way and we might have to trample your grandfathers a little. But let us express our pain, otherwise you'll forever be at war in your decapitated nations.'
 Or: 'Time to open your ears and be quiet. All in good time, and our time has come.'

In short, feel like banging on the walls of museums where our differences are displayed in stucco, schlock and ivory plastic. In short, feel like punching the talking heads yelling on the TV screens in the kebab shops that open onto the street.

How much longer will we tolerate this hell?

There's a debate about knocking down statues. Personally, I don't give a damn about your sacrosanct collective memory. I wish I had a bulldozer so I could smash the bronze faces of the men who wanted to civilise mine.

A fleeting desire that always comes back, it has roots. To say what I am, to scream aloud our rage, but on my own. Not with anyone or for anyone, and not the way people want me to say it, or think I should say it.

Say it to myself in that liminal space between fraternisation and forgetting, say it five times a day the way I say that peace will come, the awaited peace, the imagined peace, a vast plain of solutions . . .

So, shave my head and make a pact between myself and the world and the background hum of the news. I do it, I feel new. My black curls falling onto the floor, the grating of clippers against my skin. I learn that my head is flat at the back. I touch it gently. The few millimetres of hair that remain are coarse. They push up robustly from my scalp. I'm born again.

Dig a tunnel of pleasures, because I have the right and the duty and the imagination and the freedom and the desire to do so.

My violent urges have disappeared. It's my mother who helped me get rid of them. One day, after a long silence, she says, 'You're just like your father. Driven by the same rage.'

I tell myself the classic 'I don't want to end up like him.' And it works.

Even my father has calmed down. He no longer has that simmering something inside of him that led to slaps in the face and holes in the wall.

I don't know if it's age softening him, or the wisdom that comes with it.

I think that he learned, that he understood. Now it's his tenderness that comes through.

He's something to see, my father. The whole family nourished by his success.

He tells me it's natural, that it's about giving. I can see that all that omnipresent responsibility isn't easy. He's the eldest son. It's his duty to respond to the needs and whims of every member of my family. And often, in their minds, a due.

The self-sacrificing generosity, the relentless barrage of demands, I still don't understand what he expects but it's no longer my burden to carry. When I look at him, it's with empathy.

Paris carries me but I have an idiotic desire to go beyond its streets and gutters. Glide towards the sea in my white Peugeot 208. The car's filthy but I love it.

I want to return to the waves and the summer, to the burning heat between the *all-is-forbidden* of before and the *all-is-(finally)-permitted*. It's spring and for the first time, it feels like a renewal.

And then one day, when I'm perfectly fine in my new lightness of being, a friend asks me, 'Have you ever met S.?'
    'No.'
    'Really? You don't know him?'
    'Oh yeah, I do actually.'
    'He's like you. There's something about him that reminds me of you.'
    'Maybe . . .'

He tells me again the next time, 'You should ask S. out, get a drink, chat. You guys would click for sure.'

'Okay, I will.'

In the end, S. texts me and I agree to meet him for coffee. I wait in the scorching heat, in black jeans, and in a panic I order an espresso. I don't know what I'm saying anymore and I can already feel beads of sweat forming on my forehead.

He arrives wearing light-coloured shorts and a blue button-up open over a white vest. There's a cigarette hole in his sleeve. Later I'll learn that it's just happened and he's embarrassed that I notice. That's the second thing I see, after his face that makes me think: I've never seen a face like that. Not in real life, not on the Internet.

I'm really hot, I can feel something happening, which only quickens the beating of my heart, uncontrollable between my ribs. I can't think anymore, I can only nod, furrow my brows, tilt my head to the side. He doesn't seem to realise but I'm somewhere else entirely.

Boulevard de Ménilmontant. I say little.
     I find the ease with which S. talks about himself disconcerting and reassuring.
     We walk across Paris and don't notice our legs getting tired, the anaesthesia of when you like someone. An unfamiliar languor stirring, I can tell already.

It's through the first words he says to me, through that way he has of leading the conversation, something my shyness prevents me from doing, that I realise he's handsome.

The first night, I don't sleep with him. My body has been rendered impotent by the unprecedented back and forth of our voices and his soft hands all over me. I don't get hard. I'm too embarrassed to stay. I feel overtaken by this new apparition in my life: Love. In any case, I never sleep over, on principle.

On my way home that night, I fall off my bike. A small deep wound has appeared on my right calf. I put on a plaster and go to bed.

In the days that follow, I start to think: I want to see him again. I want to wash S.'s hair in the shower. His frothy, curly hair that water struggles to penetrate. Touch his stubbly chin, press my face under his arms, into his crotch, and bite his back.

In the span of a few hours, I miss him. My friends no longer hold any interest. I have nothing to tell them besides sex and cuddling, and I can see it bores them. I'm just as tired of hearing about their lives.

I'm despondent when he doesn't answer.

And then I make a choice. I promise myself and Allah that I will be vulnerable, that I will let myself be captured – prey. I will welcome my general apprehension, my uncertainty and my shyness.

I try. I do my best to be funny and agreeable. In the sheer boredom of my days, I unearth events worthy of interest to talk about on our next date. I need to seduce him. It's not a conscious decision, my brain is the one looking for pretty things to tell him about the next time. I'm obsessed by the thought that he hasn't fallen in love with me yet. I can tell he's fond of me, that he wants to reduce the time that passes between our moments together, but for now, he doesn't love me. The thought burns in my stomach before I fall asleep. I hear my own voice in my head: this will end badly.

But I can't help myself. The constant desire to eat his belly, to feel his foot on mine in the silence of the night, to lick that foot, to lick his fingers and to place my cock, when he's smoking, on his neck or arse.

In the beginning, we only talk about things we know we both know about, we drink wine and smoke large quantities of cigarettes. Then, little by little, we allow ourselves silence, nights during which it's our hands and our limbs that do the talking.

I see, writing this, his white smile, and my sperm on his gleaming statue's face. He's kneeling beneath me in the living room, the cat's eating its food, ignoring us. I don't know how I came. I wasn't there a few seconds before, I was in my dead desire. And then, he looks at me over his Grecian nose and I don't know where I went.

In love, still, that gaping hole that swallows all that is good.

A sleep of total oblivion that regenerates in a few hours. A feeling of lightness in my lungs that slowly spreads to my stomach and becomes a caress. It's a warm, humid morning in Paris and I'm walking to an appointment. I think about my night. My face is perspiring and the sweat mixes with the smell of the streets. I missed this. I make up a life in which I live here in the city, and in the house at the edge of the woods, and in the apartment overlooking Tangiers. Everything comes together.

There's still that hollow feeling in my heart, but I mask it a little. I don't want to waste this time on bitterness.

I kiss him on the nape of his neck and he rubs my ears with the palms of his hands. These are our typical gestures of affection, along with variations, gentler or with our teeth or a clenched fist, that we dole out assiduously and without a second thought.

While others are losing their minds around us, while the uproar in France swells, the hollow between my ribs fills, surely.

I still remember his silhouette in the morning. Skin peeling on his shoulders, from the sun that burnt his white body all summer, tickling the tips of my fingers. My leg is on top of the blanket, it's hot. The skin along my side, my thigh, and my shin follows the skin along his back and arse. On my right calf, a purple scar throbs. The wound didn't close properly. It's swollen and itchy.

He turns over, wakes up. He looks at my face and pinching my lips hard between his fingers, says, 'I want to eat them.'

This moment makes me want to melt, slide across the bed, soak the sheets, turn into a big puddle on the floor . . .

Maybe take the stairs to the mezzanine and end up on the velvet divan where the cat sleeps.

Often, amidst all this love and my rediscovered joy, I take the metro to the Montparnasse train station. I want to go home, reconnect with my parents. Almost imperceptibly, over time, these visits filled with silences and sideways glances have become gentler.

One day, standing in front of the screen hanging in the large concourse, I see: 'Delay thirty minutes.'

Irritated, I pace in circles. As my eyes get lost in the ceaseless bustle of people passing by, the hideous faces that follow a nice arse held up by a pair of polyester joggers, I notice a narrow staircase to the left of platform one. At the top, a glimpse of branches and a piece of sky. I make my way up slowly, like a would-be intruder. I pass an SNCF employee; he smiles at me. It would appear that I'm allowed to take these stairs.

At the top, the Jardin Atlantique. It's just rained and the sun is hitting the drops of water blanketing the leaves and the grass of the lawn. I look for somewhere to sit. Around the park, buildings form a large rectangle of offices. Beneath the park, the station, the noisy mass of trains and travellers. I've never been here before. I stretch out on a cement bench.

Sluggishness and nerves in my stomach when I think about going home. Every time I take the train leaving Paris, it's the same feeling in my body.

An insistent gaze tears me from my thoughts. I look but at first I don't see anyone near me. And then, between the bamboos at the end of a path, there's a figure. The man stares at me, an eagerness on his face that I don't recognise. He walks away. I stand up, intrigued. Another figure follows him, walks under a little footbridge. And then another guy, younger, my age at most, passes under the bridge too, giving me a furtive look.

The smell of sex, an entire world trembles in my loins.

I go closer. Public restrooms. Three of them facing the urinals.

So these secret places still exist. The guy in the middle, his face at an angle, seductive lips. But I don't go in. I watch them for a moment, their hand motions leave little to the imagination. I can't see much but I guess.

I think about S. whom I'm leaving for the week.

The guy on the far left, in his fifties, face marked with rosacea, turns towards me. He shows me his dick. I smile. In any case, it's time to catch my train. I take another second to observe their shadows in the gloom of the public urinals. The first guy turns back around and they start touching one another. I realise that watching them doesn't interest me. I take the stairs back to the station concourse.

Barely seated in the train: a voice over the loudspeaker. Another delay. This gives me more time to think about my relationship with my family. Everyone seems exhausted by resentment, and in the orange glow of the TGV I tell myself that maybe reconciliation doesn't always taste good. It might be a little sour.

When I arrive, we go for a bike ride. On the way back, I let the wind slide across my face, and I half-shut my eyes, taking care to stay in the centre of the deserted street, behind my father. I try to get rid of the sensation in my knotted throat. I wobble a little, it's a nice day, and I think about how to make the bitterness I have towards him dissipate.

The next day: salted butter dripping down our chins as we listen to a terrible story from the neighbour. The cats are lying together in the sun. The son of someone in town lost his arm to a car window, ripped off when he crashed into a telegraph pole. My mother is horrified. My father whispers a prayer. We continue gorging ourselves on oranges and croissants. I can tell peace has settled in. I can see that despite the toxic climate around us, the world has given me a small chance to grab: find harmony with my parents.

I think of loads of things that don't come out. I don't organise my thoughts, I don't express anything aloud. I keep it all for me as I watch them. I wish I could tell them how happy S. and I are, that my anxiety has quieted.

S. says, 'Lots of times, it's when we speak without thinking that ideas come to us, that things happen.'
    I respond, 'Sometimes the truth is better left unsaid.'

We were brought up so differently. S. also says, 'You should tell your father about your life. Tell him about me.'
    I respond, 'Sometimes the truth is better left unsaid.'

Our realities are on opposite ends of the spectrum.

It's true, though, I admit: my father no longer seems to be fanning the flames that once incinerated my poetry and my secrets. A large drawbridge has lowered between us, and we look at each other with new curiosity. On the patio, in the approaching spring, everyone's sharing anecdotes, things they saw or heard somewhere. I listen and tell myself that the time for secrets has passed. And yet, with self-awareness comes the realisation that you never really wanted to know who you were at the edge of that brambly terrain. It comes with the understanding that you were always trying to escape the insipid warmth of blood ties. All that lost time to make up for. I think that for him it's normal – the distance from me, the money he sends me, the rare, cautious questions.

One morning, we all pick blackberries together at the back of the garden, along a wall blackened by rain. Of course, I stain my T-shirt. Then we go inside and my mother rinses the berries thoroughly in the sink. My father is lavishing laughter on my sister and brother seated around the dining table. I watch them, I smile, I say nothing. The patio doors are open to the blooming garden, illuminating the three of them. It's a beautiful scene that smells of sugar. My mother boils the blackberries. 'Let's make jam!' she exclaims, suddenly content. They're talking about anything, about nothing, it's pleasant. My father looks at me, interested in my opinion. This is the denouement. We pour sugar into the smashed, scalding fruit. We take turns mixing, pretending it's a contest. Time to seal the jars. Everyone scatters, somewhere in the house or garden while the fruit mixture rests. Calm returns.

S. often says, 'The silence in your family isn't about reserve, it's about taboo.'
     And I say, 'You have no idea what you're talking about. Sometimes the truth is better left unsaid.'

My adult body in the doorway, eyes up and filled with the beautiful things I've seen and them, stunned to silence, happy, in a way, that I'm back. My visits bear fruit. The weather gets better, the sky clears.

I have my golden *khamsa* in the hollow of my clavicles, and now I move through the world certain of loving thick hands and knotty thighs. I come from a nameless tribe, Jeddi left without telling us.

It's a subject of which no one speaks in my family. Ever since I was a little boy, I've heard voices whispering the same question: 'Why does Jeddi get tears in his eyes when someone asks about his mountain?'

But at the same time, they know. Collective denial or else a shared intuition.

I gather the information I can find, my cousins do too, searching for the reasons for his exile. Because before fleeing to France, there was another departure – from his clan. We have no idea, no clue, we imagine the colonial police at his heels. We add barbed-wire tattoos to his old-man arms and imagine him a thief. One hundred years of secrets are locked inside his ever-proud body, behind his face so gentle with children and so harsh with adults.

The day after his death, on a car ride through France's marshlands, my father drops, 'It was a crime of honour . . . You know, the snowball effect . . . He wasn't safe anymore . . . An eye for an eye was still the law . . . Probably still is for that matter . . . We can never set foot there.'

Through his halting speech, his half-sentences that create a torrent of words interrupted by the things that can't be said, are impossible to say, I understand.

My golden *khamsa* nestles in the hollow of my clavicles. From now on nothing affects me. I move through the world, sure that I love brown-haired caresses and smiling moustaches. I exist, certain that I'm the son of Mohamed, himself the son of Mohamed, himself *ould Ali*.

I should add my grandmother's shifting eyes on me. She's age-
ing too fast but I find her in my memories. I'm a child and her
hand is resting on the back of my damp neck. She's whispering
words in my ear. The beginning of a successful conquest, it
turns out.

Revealed scraps and eternal secrets act as a fermenting agent: I
come to terms with myself. I'm not the only one sifting through
the stories of a chaotic legacy.

'Diaspora kids are so cringe,' says a friend.

But then there's that incredible faculty given us to step outside of our culture and take root elsewhere, otherwise, however
we like. I tell myself that the diaspora is like a great flock of
chimeras. People who have kids and teach them you can never go home again and those same people who have other kids
and tell them, 'I don't know who we are. Figure it out. Invent
something.'

A whole horizon of possibilities. Things are changing, the world
diversifying, go on, come into your own. Our embarrassed parents watching on and people back home smiling at our awk-
ward gestures and mispronounced words. So yes, we have to
collectively endure the weight of an entire country bearing
down on us, but isn't that the beauty of it? We sprout across
France regardless, we invent ways to show our nativeness and
that we're the future, both at the same time.

Likewise, take wing, take root, without the irrigation of language, not sure of anything. My second cousin insists, 'I'm not
Arab, I'm French. I'm a French Muslim of Moroccan origin.'

She's ten years old and wants to prove herself like everyone
else. Our beliefs are quite the feat. Already convinced, in the
innocence of youth, that one's allegiances need to be sorted,
made presentable. See what a country demands of you and make

yourself small accordingly, shake loose any words that might put you in a box. So young but trying to justify her presence here. Legitimising her small girl's body by using words that tower above her.

I take a good look at myself, a good look at my brother and sister and everyone else, and all of us, every last one, make sense. I see us in the family house with its open windows and all of us, every last one, are precisely where we should be.

On the train back, I have a smile on my lips. Spring sprawls across the city parks, and in the courtyard of the building I see birds and slugs. My life softens a little more, thanks to all my remembering.

Quick enough, the apartment fills with heat. June settles in and I can't stay still. I want to see something new, get away, glimpse the horizon. Paris is suffocating my newly gained bliss.

I cross the country on the A6, a.k.a. the 'sun motorway', in my beaten-up Peugeot 208. I feel at home in that car. The left rearview mirror fell off and I had to attach it with duct tape. I see a nuclear power station along the route to Marseille and deer leaping through rolling valleys. I wonder: How did man permanently terrorise all that's living? And also: Why do dogs put up with our presence?

When I would hold a captured field mouse or a swallow in my hands. Looking at their skin, their eyes, their black claws . . .

How does the world teach children about their power?
　　Why must we hurt to understand how pain works?
　　I used to think: I wish animals weren't so afraid of me. I still think that.
　　Why do we have to hide to observe wildlife in the forests and at lakeshores?
　　How did the DNA of animals retain the lesson?

I listen to people debating the world on the radio. The sound either crackles or is perfectly clear. I'm indifferent, I let all my random ideas emerge and I feel revived by the drive. The succession of cypress trees and the surge of cars makes me smile. I'm going in the right direction: south.

The countryside smells like warm grass, whiffs of vegetation fill the nose. Emotions quicken and voilà, summer's here. In the south, summers are intense and welcoming, straight out of a novel.

Beside the dehydrated shrubs, I hear them say, 'The heatwave will ravage the country from June to August.' A cliff of white rocks and my friends who take offense at nothings. Whining and moaning, engrossed in bickering over inanities. But they can say whatever they want, too. I'm not really here. I'm in the denouement in progress, in the reconciliation that's beginning.

Midday slump and orgeat syrup, ice cubes in the coffee, I'm mainly thinking about his mouth biting my neck still warm from the sun. The iodine remains in S.'s hair all day and night. In the dark, he clings to my chest, his legs braided with mine.

In my head, I tell him, 'I want to give you a child. I want us to scandalise the world with a hyper-innovative technique that will allow our bodies unprecedented feats. You'll conceive from a blend of our ejaculations. Something will grow in your belly, nature obliging, and you'll bring a baby into the world for the two of us. I'm so filled with longing for you that I could steal a kid off the street and say it's ours.'

He tells me, in the bedroom with the lights off, 'I don't ever want to get married.'

But I don't care about the dress or the suit or the detached house or the sea, couldn't care less. I want to plant my seed filled with love in your body unable to receive it.

And for a miracle to make it work. Raising a child doesn't interest me, just to be clear. It's simply for the beauty of the act. He whispers, 'One day, I'd like to be a dad . . .'

Come on then! Let's merge to create a perfect offspring inside your belly. I want to deform your skin and bring forth a little person with both our faces.

To hell with the sceptics, I want a scientific revolution. You would give me a sublime child.

As I'm thinking about my insane idea, the conversation among my sunbathing friends gets heated. It happens, it's part of the game.

I remind E., 'You can't spend your whole life being angry . . .'

J., bright red, interrupts, 'If you had read the IPCC report, you'd know there's no point discussing the future.'

No one's surprised, we just look at each other. We're all perfectly aware of the omnipresent catastrophe, already in progress, looming above us as we drink ginger lemonade, chests bare, and discuss the refugees at the bottom of the Mediterranean.

We're perfectly aware of the catastrophe and I think about where I grew up and say thank you.

Thank you for the calm and the privilege of growing up surrounded by trees.

I like the heat; my anxiety dissipates. In the paradise of my dreams, I see crevasses filled with desire and roots that plunge into a pond of joy.

Loving is long, it's like opening the magic silver shell of an oyster. A dagger in my purple heart brimming with hope.

The closeness between S. and me is like cement poured into a mould of our fears. The ingredients: my dead anxiety and a juvenile faith.

Our language is like elvish chants or a recitation from the Quran, incredible to someone who doesn't believe in magic.

I feel safe. I smell him everywhere I go: in the soil and on a crust of bread, in the wool of a scratchy blanket and in the middle of a sodden street.

Suddenly, I imagine him loving other boys and it's a punch to the jaw. Jealousy from the depths, it's never come to the surface before, I'm discovering it now.

He reveals, 'A lover gave me that plant.'

He repeats himself, tells me a few times, and always enthusiastically. I know the story by heart: after they had sex, the guy gave him a shoot. S. took it home, planted it in a pot, and now here it is growing on his window sill.

One day, S. is in the shower and I look at the plant. I grab a leaf and tear it off, then crush it in my palm. Relief. I decide to go for it. I pour a handful of salt on the potting soil around the plant. I take the jug of water from the coffee table and empty it into the pot. I put a smile back on my face and sit on the small velvet couch, calmly waiting for S. to finish.

During a conversation, a few days later, he whispers: 'You never get jealous. It's annoying.'

Behind him, I see the brown leaves starting to fall. I smile, teeth clenched.

Another time, he trimmed the hair blanketing his chest and stomach. It reveals his body and gives him a different silhouette. I feel like I'm discovering him anew.

As I put my mouth on him, I say, 'It's like you're a new man.'

He frowns, 'You were sick of the old one?'

I roll my eyes. Apart from this mild bickering, it's all bliss and harmony. Round-trip ticket, Paris, the sea, the countryside, happiness.

I encourage my girlfriends with bouquets of flowers. My friends and their flowers, so beautiful together. Simple gestures amid my bliss, my fears, and sunny terraces.

I whisper to S., 'All I've ever wanted was to be left alone.'

And him, 'We all have a dream . . .'

During a stroll (now I walk alone when I really need to air out my mind), I notice a shack in the Bois de Vincennes.

Why not hide out in there for a few seconds? Why not lie down in there forever?

The brown, dead tissues fallen from the branches might make a nice bed, no? Except: it's time to build a life . . .

We drink and we eat in the sun and that's pretty much it, in the paradise of my dreams.

I was born a few hours away from being a Libra, the sign of balance. I never could bear to decide. S. says, 'Seventeen hours away from your true nature . . .'

I wait on the metro platform, on my way back from the park, and I feel something tickling my neck. I reach up and, on my finger, a ladybird. Poor thing. There were tons of them in the gardens. Red ones, yellow ones, black ones with red spots.

I coax it into the palm of my hand and close my fingers. Now it's my prisoner. I don't want it to fly into the dark metro tunnels and never find its way out.

It must have crawled onto my T-shirt when I came into Gambetta station.

I keep it in my damp hand so it doesn't fly away. I don't want it to die.

I remember that ladybirds secrete a brownish, foul-smelling liquid when threatened. I slowly open my hand, I'm standing, surrounded by bodies packed into the carriage.

I see that it's waiting on my skin, not a drop of the repulsive excretion. It's patient, it understands.

Ladybirds used to lay their oval eggs along our low garden wall. The eggs would turn into strange larvae, grey but covered with symmetrical orange pustules along their abdomens.
 Both larvae and ladybirds eat aphids.

Suddenly my obsession for insects returns. Why did I bury my love of bugs? I should have become a biologist.

The black ones with red spots are cannibals, I think. Or maybe that's a legend spread through playgrounds and back gardens. The kind of false or distorted information you say when there are no grown-ups around and that you continue to believe for a long time.

I exit the metro. A bright day. I raise my index finger, the ladybird climbs up and, of course, flies away. I hope it finds some more greenery here at the other end of Paris.

The summer holidays stretch on. A parallel world in which things don't matter the same.

A black river gliding along a bed of green stones, the water is freezing and we've been walking for a long time, our shoulders sore and exhausted from our backpacks.

My girlfriends are no longer in love and ruin the trip for everyone else. We went out for a walk, and one of them decided to stay behind in the stone house. The other one doesn't say a word about the sublime hills stretching before us.

'It's really a shame,' says E. But I'm cruel and bored in the southern heat, I think it's rather entertaining. They avoid each other from room to room and, at night, sleep together.

One of them tells me, 'Thank god the bed is enormous . . .'

It's a perfectly normal-sized bed. I wonder if they're lying to us about their imminent breakup.

She grumbles, 'If she would stop doing so many drugs, if she would sleep at night, if she would stop cheating on me, if . . .'

Golden vistas and a winding path through young willow trees.

We're naked in the gentle water. It's a bit of a cliché but it feels nice.

Hibiscus tea, but they don't seem any calmer.
	They look at each other with daggers in their eyes at every meal. True, it is kind of a shame . . .

But I'm thinking about S., again. I have a bruise on my skin in the shape of his mouth. Joy up to my eye sockets.

He told me that he worshiped werewolves and vampires when he was little. About all the films he would watch in search of new images of the mythical creatures. He admits to me that his quest had an erotic element. I wish I could grow fur on my shoulders or make my canines bigger. I imagine myself turning into a brutal, salivating monster and capturing him. Sucking his blood and clawing his back.

At night, when I'm alone, I want to plug into the thousands of possibilities offered by this hellfire of a world. In my dreams, I swallow my fear and I feed the void with fruits, words, affection and choices. I can sense harmony settling in. The smile stretching across my face when I walk into my family home is sincere.

I shake myself and summer is over. Goodbye south of France. I return to Paris and move into a new apartment.

Cocaine, impossible to sleep, my new place too unfamiliar. It smells like plaster dust and the sweat of the men who renovated it and the white paint on the walls. I watch sparrows fighting and copulating out my bedroom window. This is the bed from when I was a teenager, I had it brought here. I tell myself: I slept in this bed nearly my whole life. I still hear the party in my head, and thoughts flash through my mind. They're blank thoughts, which light up my brain but don't leave any trace. I can taste the alcohol on my palate. I get out of bed to make fruit juice. I wait as the machine crushes the flesh of strawberries and apples.

My neighbour yells in a language I don't understand. Yiddish I think. I listen, frozen like an animal outside its territory.

Shit. I threw the freshly made juice into the stainless-steel sink. I wasn't thinking, I poured it out with the fruit peels. I drank nothing, absence. I calculate in my head: 4.50 euros for the strawberries + 3 euros for the apples + ginger = I'm an idiot.

It's funny, the places we live are an extension of our private-most lives but are built from such rigid materials. The volatility of our insides versus the hyper-resistance of a bedroom door. I think about the workmen who broke down the dividing wall between the kitchen and the living room. Now, I go from the sink to the couch naked, gliding along the hardwood floor.

Houses should be more malleable. Modular, flexible, with rounded corners and walls on wheels. I don't know exactly where I'm going with this. I need to get used to the apartment, and now I have the necessary enthusiasm.

It's a radiant September and we're on our way to visit Italy as a family. We're polite and pleasant to each other on the plane, and I wonder what I'm doing here. Florence. The grandiosity does us good. 'There's more dramatic than us.'

From the outset, a damp heavy heat permeates the streets and floats into the crowded cafés.

A downpour and the whole city is drenched, people dashing through grey and brown puddles. The storm has nothing to do with the impatient love sitting in my stomach, but they marry nicely for a prolonged moment (a whole day) of bliss.

Idiotically happy as we are, we decide to stop for ice cream in a café as the rain pours down and to continue visiting the ruins. And, I should add, laughing all the while. Florence is nourishing our souls, the sustenance such that you could almost believe it will last forever. That the 'before' will no longer be a defining element of our lives, that right in the middle of unhappiness there will only be the things that matter.

My father, my mother, my sister, my brother and me. It's nice, the reconciliation continues on cobblestones old as time.

Later, on the hotel balcony: Mum fell asleep in a plastic chair and Dad tells me he hates money more than anything in the world.

Italy is very beautiful and the food is delicious.

I tell things to my parents illuminated by candles on white trattoria tablecloths, crumbs prickling our bare elbows. I tell them how unhappy I was growing up. I burst into laughter when I see their faces in yellow and orange, surprised and reserved. We have adult conversations.

My father asks, 'Have you read *Le Gone du Chaâba*?' I still haven't, though he's mentioned it several times, and for the first time I think that I'd like to read it. I smile. 'As soon as you give me a copy!'

I paint them a picture of me as a child: listless, scared of failure. My mother gets upset. I smile again. 'It's in the past.'

I also confess, 'I think I know what to do with my life.' They respond in unison, surprised and enthusiastic, 'Really?'
        'I want to write. It's basically the only thing I know how to do anyway.'

They don't say anything. I don't detect any particular relief. My mother abruptly says, 'Yes, that's a very good idea.'

My father sighs, watches the crowds of people walk past the restaurant terrace lit up by paper lanterns. He goes, 'You'll have to let us read what you write . . .'

I mumble a yes.

That night, on the hotel bed, I wonder if I'm overdoing it. I wonder whether making my happiness dependant on my family's approval is a step backwards. In the dim bedroom light, I rub the palm of my hand against my shaved head and tell myself: you think too much.

And then there's more strolling through the streets of Florence. There's my father behind me, clearly embarrassed by me gazing at David versus Goliath, his extraordinary body, his foot level with my face, a monster of beauty.

I see myself in the hotel lift: the sun has healed my skin and covered up the signs of sadness. For a few months, I've sensed a layer of tissue, fat and muscle discreetly forming along my ribs. I'm gradually getting bigger, I can tell from my T-shirt, which doesn't fit the same. My body long trapped in a cage of thinness, hollows in my thighs, seems to be saying something different now. It's getting comfortable, getting used to my calmer mind.

The hushed, languid song of the turtle dove accompanying our voices. We're talking beneath the trees in a little square whose name I've forgotten. By the end, I'm standing with my back to the café, where the others are waiting. I'm facing the square, its fountain, its mischievous pigeons. Dad leans on my shoulder. 'I'm happy. Your life seems like it's going well.'

For once he puts his hand on me and I don't take a step back, I don't jump.

We wander all day in the heatwave, the sun beating down on our foreheads and leaving red welts on our necks. My brother wishes he was more resistant, his skin less pale. He says, 'Nobody ever makes the connection between my last name and my weird face.'

He runs his hand through his straight, sun-kissed hair. He's right, you would never guess. I think about my rage and my misgivings. I tell myself that it's all been largely diluted. With my new faith, my new freedom, I sense that everything's mixed together. The fear of picking a side is gone.

We keep walking, sticking to the shade, hugging the stone walls, and at one point, as we're walking single-file, I say, 'I'm going to get my Moroccan identity card.'

Everyone turns towards me; I'm the last in the line. It feels like torture every time we stop between two museums or on the way to a restaurant, the heat suffocating.

They look at me. My mother is troubled. My brother furrows his brows, I doubt the idea ever occurred to him. My sister nods. She wants to get hers too, she says. My father: 'It's not the same for you, L. But you, my boy, you don't need it.'

He lets the silence hold. Then he adds, 'It's too dangerous.'

Time drags after that. We continue walking and I wonder what he means. Or rather, I know perfectly well what he means but I'm surprised that he publicly acknowledged that I'm different.

The temperature rises a few degrees, reaches the limit of what's bearable. On edge in the heat, we're all a little more cautious, precisely to avoid shattering our beautiful harmony. I'm mildly annoyed. I thought getting my Moroccan green card was a nice idea.

The final two nights: no sleep, an image of the document in my mind.

The final day, I think: I listen to my father, I can hear him tell me things about his past. His opinion doesn't make me sick anymore. I'm starting to be able to look at him without wanting to punch a wall, hard with two clenched fists.

We have conversations in the narrow streets of Florence, which starts to feel artificial after a while. It's true, all that beauty, in the end, keeps you from noticing.

My voice still trembles a little around the others. I'm tired of the bitter taste that lingers in my mouth and seeps into my happiness at slowly but surely becoming myself. My mother tells me, 'You ought to appreciate your shyness. It stops you from talking nonsense.'

She tells me that in the plane and I look out the window. The sea is everywhere, a swathe of silk, and the chaos of the waves at this distance offers mild comfort. I mumble, 'Yeah, well, sometimes the truth is better left unsaid . . .'

And her: 'No, that's not what I meant. When you're sure of something, when you believe in it very strongly, you should say it.'

Engines roaring under the wing, the cabin trembles and the seat belt lights go on.

Me: 'I don't blame him.'

She gives me a long look and starts to say something but the plane shakes so hard that she can't talk. Immediately after the turbulence, she says, 'Tell him.'

We return to the house in which I grew up.

I'm tanning in the garden in my tight black cotton briefs, one leg raised, like a girl.

My father is on the other side of the patio, near the pool.

He's yelling into the telephone, his hands raised. It looks like he's about to commit hara-kiri.

I no longer feel *hshouma*, not really. Our relationship has been liveable for a while now.

I tell myself: he's crazy, just like me. When he doesn't know how to love me anymore, he grabs things and sets them on fire. I'm the same, I throw things at the wall occasionally. But ultimately, I can heal from all of that.

I look at the stone patio flooded with light.

I do a little dance. He's hung up, he sees me but says nothing . . . Now, my father and I live and let live.

S. says that I'm afraid of my father. He says I should confront him, that he doesn't deserve everyone fussing over him. He apologises as he says it. I know he's angry alongside me, on my behalf. He can't understand my family culture, how we do things over there, all of us. But I see my father and feel compassion. My memories are still loud and vengeful but I sense some kind of meaning burgeoning.

He didn't fail to teach me Arabic for want of trying. That's very clear to me now. Resistant as I was, he tried to make me see what I was rejecting. He attempted to show me the whole picture of where I came from. He didn't give up out of laziness or weakness before a society dominated by French, before my mother who at night whispered words in my ear that certainly weren't in Darija.

Exile first, then the dismembering machine of assimilation. Of course he couldn't give us something he could no longer find deep in his chest or in his threadbare memories.

His memorial mechanisms altered, he feels idiotic whenever he tries to describe his youth 'beneath the fig trees', as he puts it.

My father began writing, messy heaps of words that don't respect the rules of grammar.

I read them, stunned to discover what I've known since I was little. On the inside, he's burning alive. His memories from Morocco are recounted haphazardly, always from before the exile. It's paradise on earth, there are good guys and bad guys. The adults are faceless figures floating above the world of children.

He hardly mentions violence. I know there was violence.

I inherited his hatred and his love for his past. The big secret that his father left him, too. I've only ever heard whispers about my jeddi. His tribe, up in the mountains, suddenly wanted nothing more to do with him. He was forced to leave, to abandon his wife and son. My family is the fruit of his second life.

I see the reason for the silence, for the holes in the story. In my mind, when I think about my grandfather and my father, about the cause of their broken memories, I see this: there's blood on a wall.

Staying in his native village would have meant dying in his turn.

My grandfather decided to flee.

A parallel of secrecy, my father says the same thing every time I ask: 'I've forgotten, I've forgotten, I've forgotten.'

Ever since his father departed, since Jeddi died, he's been struck by bolts of lightning, memories returning.

I wait for his writings, I encourage his reflections. I read his words that describe a perfect age when adults are nothing more than hands on your neck and benevolent voices.

Today, I felt something run dry inside my chest. I think that's what's keeping me standing. I think I've stopped deviating. A few interlocking pieces of the story keep running through my head.

I think about the houses my father constructs on damp lots where I used to play as a kid. I don't say anything to him, there's work to be done. I'm no longer angry enough. Not quite so sensitive. Before, I would cry for an entire day if I found a mole trap or happened upon my uncle decapitating a snake.

Now, my father and I live and let live.

I can picture the imposing mimosa tree, a colossus of branches and yellow flowers, that had to be cut down. The saga still etched into my chest, though, when I think about it, beside the big front gate, its shoots grew into a new tree, as massive as the previous one.

So yes, when it comes down to it, I can heal from all of this.

Wednesday, 16 March. WhatsApp message: 'She's gone.'

The train, a thick, liquid sleep, no dreams. My brother snoring on my shoulder. And immediately, starting at the Paris station, this thought: I'm sorry, *smahli*, for not being able to talk to you. I didn't learn how to speak to you in your language, our language, in time. I find you in a complex of industrial-looking buildings. The car's parked and I get out in the middle of nothing at all, in that awful hospital complex that I don't care to describe. I walk up to the door. It's locked, which puts me straight away in a terrible mood.

Let me in. My aunts are inside, they've washed your body. S. said, 'I could never do that.' But I'd have loved to. To honour you, I mean. To reach a level of deep, total intimacy beyond the language for which I never made enough of an effort.

Our minds come from two distinct worlds. S. and me, I mean.

The morgue corridor. Everyone waiting in the stillness of grief, glued to the walls, eyes politely averted from each other's pain. My mother says, 'That smell will haunt me.' I don't smell anything. My father and my uncles enter the room to lift your body and put it in its box. I see the door reopen and it's our turn. My aunt's eyes are dry, her hands open as if she's holding the holy book. That's what I see first, everyone praying together. The room fills with people who've come to see you. I look at the end of the open casket but I don't let my gaze travel to your face. Before this, in the twenty-four hours between my arrival and this moment, I'm at your house and I don't understand that you're dead. I see your children and grandchildren in the same spots, sitting at the same tables. I see your bed in your room and I don't understand why everyone's panicking. I tell myself that you're still here, in a way, as long as we don't make a fuss, as long as we all act as if nothing has happened.

Now it's time to step forward and enter the room, let my gaze follow everyone else's. Tears form immediately. One at a time, it's time to step up and say goodbye. There's no avoiding it. I have to make my way to the coffin and see you in your shroud. Around me, I hear people reciting, asking that the gates of paradise open for you. I imagine two large arched gates topped with ivory spikes, for those with duplicitous intentions. Your skin is ice-cold and very soft. I say: '*Bslama 3lik*,' and thank you for all your strength and all your resilience and all your kisses and gentle hugs. Thank you for the milk that came from your body to feed my father, his brothers and sisters, and your newborns who didn't survive. Thank you. Thank you. And I'm sorry. Thank you for using your back to push away the suffering of the world to build your family, for the chaos you held at bay as much as you could. I'm sorry for the dispossession and exile France inflicted on you. *Shukran* or *smahli* for all the stories you told and that will be passed down to me somehow, in French, later. Thank you for fighting poverty by giving magic keys to your sons and daughters to open the world for us. To offer it to us.

I think this is when I leave my mind. I walk through my family praying in a circle, I keep going. No one follows me, I keep going. I reach the waiting room. There's a filthy aquarium in which float three orange fish with black eyes. I watch them, hand on my chest, I press hard. I think that I don't understand what your leaving means for me. I'm having trouble breathing. Your death comes nearly one year after Jeddi's. It's as if the possibility of making you both proud is vanishing too. I wait there, listening to my family's muffled, forbidden sobs in the room at the end of the corridor. You mustn't cry too loud over the dead, repeats my uncle. This lasts a long time. When it's over, I gently stand with the sensation of having lost something. As I write these words, tears in my eyes, I feel like I've mislaid something very important, like I forgot to get dressed. And almost immediately, the instant I walk out of that lifeless hospital blanketed in beige, the missing settles in.

Thick haze. Second round. Pack a suitcase. Sleep on the *7aifas* under a table. Cold, alone on the floor, in the bedroom commandeered to welcome visitors the next day. Recitations from the Quran. Open house, again. Then wait for the plane. Laugh idiotically with my cousins, huge bags under my eyes, exhausted by the violence of grief. Wander Orly Airport. Tangiers tarmac, awful repetition.

I go through customs and I'm angry. I say, 'Bonjour.' He says, '*Nta maghribi?*' You're of Moroccan origin? And me, anticipating the question, 'I don't have an ID card.' I hold out the death certificate. I'm tired and don't feel like proving anything to anyone. We go through. A litany of memories, everyone recounts a moment with her, about her. Everyone carefully guarding their little secrets. My head, though, is throbbing with silence. I don't know. There's five or six of us on the bed, taking turns sharing things we remember. And suddenly I jump in, I tell them what I remember: her hands. I tell them, 'We had the same hands.' She said so once. Her hand patting me on the back to get me to sleep when I was a little boy, her hand on the nape of my neck, her hand scratching my head resting on her knees. Just last week, it feels like. Her long fingers and large palms, like mine.

The next day at dawn: rays of light stretching across their heads, they all bent down a split second before me.
I know how but I'm not in the habit.
Foreheads against the shared rug, the sun rises behind the imam who says so many things. *Salat al-janazah.* Fast. I don't have time to pray for you. There's not a single moment after my *surah* to speak to you, it goes too quickly.

I don't understand all the words. My sister tells me, 'Maybe it's for the best . . .' But she doesn't know the magic in the glimmering shards of olive-green and blue glass planted along the mosque's white cement wall. She doesn't know the communion of hopes and sorrows in the heart of the city of Tangiers, and the importance it imparts on daily life. A sermon full of words I don't understand, and it's being passed on to me. My father trembles, he touches my shoulders.

Someone has us pose beneath the wisteria before the mosque door. My father is moved. Absurd; he doesn't believe in God. It feels like a grand denouement. By the end, the sun is high and white. Everyone rose a split second before me. I don't know how I'm supposed to embrace my neighbour. Arms behind my back, cheeks damp, it's a new day and the imam stops speaking.

I tap my heel on the carpet of the hire car, stuck in traffic. The ambulance carrying the coffin that was waiting in the mosque during the prayer flies through the city and we're trapped behind. It takes forever. I'm sweating. Finally, my father swerves into a narrow street and gets us to our destination. High on the hill, I see the coffin already advancing. They can't wait, not even a son can stop the march to the grave. My father yells, 'Run!'

The car door opens and without thinking, I race up the hill, sprinting between the graves in a white *qamis*. I climb the hill same way I did last year, grief a cycle. I'm there to hold the rope that lowers you into the ground. My father arrives and jumps into the grave. He places his hand on the wood. The others scream at him to stop, he's hindering the religiously established sequence of events. I hold them back. I see his legs sinking into the dirt piling up. I think he wishes he could stay with you, be buried with you. The men around us yell again, this needs to happen as quickly as possible, it's against the rules to be buried alive with one's mother. And fair enough, it's not like he can stay there indefinitely. I grab my father's arms and with a little help, the others and I are able to get him out of the grave. He remains standing, static. I keep my eyes averted from his face. Again, like before, I dig up dirt with my fingers. We have to cover your body as quickly as possible, it's the law. The smell of clay, the cut plants sinking into the mound we made with our shovels, everything repeating. This time I'm used to it. I have more time to pray. I ask the earth and detritus to grant you a resting place. This time, however, as the palm leaves are erected and containers of water poured over the white flowers, the women approach. I'm in front of the grave, both hands open. I listen to people recite the appropriate words. And the women arrive, heads covered. I think: How lucky . . . I wish I could hide my face. Someone tells my aunt, 'You can come closer – but no crying.' She looks up, she's in the middle of the line of her sisters in front of your grave, and she retorts: 'If the Prophet could shed a tear for his son, I'm allowed.' I don't know if anyone sees me, but I smile a large, fleeting smile.

We slowly return to the house. I hand out bread stuffed with dates. There are lots of people, again. The order of the world since last year hasn't been altered. Nothing has changed.

Recitations from the Quran, men and women on their respective sides, and me on the rooftop, listening to traffic, car horns blending with the voices inside. We come here to abandon your bodies, it's forever repeating. I wonder what the statistics are for funeral repatriations. How many families per week fly from France to bury their loved ones in the earth from which they emerged?

Again, I hear dogs incessantly barking below. When I eventually have to go inside and eat dinner with everyone, my aunt digs her fingers into my shoulder, she holds me back.

She goes, 'I can't stand them anymore. All those people, all those strangers from the neighbourhood coming to give me their ridiculous condolences. What am I supposed to do with them? What could I possibly do with all those inane words?'

I can tell she's spinning out. Normally she's tightly controlled, so hard on herself that her face bears the marks. A ball of nerves.

She keeps going: 'They come and tell me that the reason my mother suffered so much was so she could reach paradise faster? I don't want to go *fi Jannah* if that's what it's like.'

And me: 'You realise they say that because they don't have anything else to say. What do they know anyway?'

Her: 'Exactly! So if they don't know, they should keep their mouths shut . . . And if it is true, I don't want to be welcomed into God's paradise, or you, or my daughters.'

She continues her blasphemy, audibly, drowning out the Quran recitations coming from a huge Sony speaker that my cousin put on a chair.

She's not done. 'It's idiotic. It's bad enough I hear it in France, every other Arab telling me the same thing. God tests those he loves? Are you serious? Why would you say that? I'm the one who told her they had to cut off her leg. I'm the one who had to tell her what the doctor was saying, who had to translate the bad news. I'm the one who carried her to death's door. I don't know where God was. I didn't see him.'

I respond, guiding her towards the balcony and away from the eager ears of scandal, 'You don't mean what you're saying. Before she stopped understanding, before she fell asleep, she believed in God. He was there, with her. Or that's how I think it works, anyway.'

She stops talking. I pray that she doesn't cry. I never know what to do when people cry. She remains impassive, looking over the railing at Tangiers. I leave her there, motionless, to think about her shattered faith.

I enter the living room and I join the men, who have begun to recite. Someone has turned off the speaker. The women are in the hallway, behind the door, heads against the wall or on a shoulder, crying amid the swell of masculine voices. I sit down and can tell a few people are looking at me: Who is he? Why does he share their grief? How does he know al-Fatiha?

But it slides off me like I'm made of oilcloth. I don't care anymore that I'm between two worlds, take it or leave it. I've been liberated from the quivering in my voice, from the endless nights spent debating which side I should pick. I'm neither one nor the other and to be honest, that suits me just fine. If France is doomed to go to rot, I'll go elsewhere. If I can never feel entirely like myself in Morocco, I'll go elsewhere. A sad story but it's not my fault. I can't fix any of it on my own.

And that same litany in my mind: I'm so sorry. *Smahli.* When I swallow the lamb tagine with cashews, I feel my throat tighten with regrets. I didn't learn your language, I couldn't talk to you except with my body and my smile. The *sadaqah* meal is obligatory, an homage. I eat and eat, every bite sticking in my throat, but I keep going. Meat, bread, glass of water, and I resume. Again in my head: *smahli.* I'm sorry, forgive me, thank you. I could only talk to you with a kiss on the forehead and a hand on your shoulder. My sister says, 'That's pretty good already.' But I still have a burning knot in my gut, which keeps me from sleeping. Once the men in hooded djellabas have left, when it's silent again, the living room is filled with bodies asleep on the *sedaris*, and meanwhile I'm staring at the orange light coming from outside, insomniac. I stay like that until dawn, I'm waiting for morning. At the first note of birdsong, the first beaks clicking, I jump up. Get outside quickly, go for a walk. For a few hours, I roam Tangiers, the city half-asleep, the air humid and smelling of dust. On the cars, dewdrops draw lines through the sheet of orange sand that covers everything. Winds brought it from the Sahara and painted the city. I see a hammam. I go inside. In the gloom, a small man gets up, smiles, he's missing three teeth.

Welcome. That'll be sixty dirhams. The place is empty, it's early still. There's a large portrait of a man I've never seen before: Moulay Hassan al-Awwal. Sultan of Morocco. I smile. In the changing room, I slowly remove my clothes: black *gandura*, black joggers, right black sock with a hole, left grey sock.

I descend into the heat.

And then, buried beneath street level, a captive of the burning steam and the semi-darkness, I burst into tears.

A man comes over, he coats my body with black soap and sits me on a bench. I'm blind and continue to weep. I sit there long enough that my head feels woozy, that my arms go limp. I don't know where he was waiting, how he senses the sensations in my body, but he returns. I don't see his face but he guides me to a large marble table. I lie down and I cry. He rubs me down briskly, and I feel my skin rolling under the exfoliation glove. He sprays me with a large jet of hot water then pats my thigh. I flip over and I see his face above me. Gaps in his teeth and wrinkles at the corners of his eyes. He rubs me down again and I continue to cry. I feel his big soft belly against my right arm. He pats me again, on the stomach, the sound echoing against the tile walls. I sit up. I cry as he stands in front of me sanding the skin on my neck, vigorously rubbing my shoulders. I smile. His movements seem so tender. He sprays lots more water on me and I can see dead skin going down the drain. He grabs shower gel. I lie down again and he washes me. I'm still crying but quietly now, I feel clean. The grief ebbs. He nudges me to stand up again, to rinse me one last time. I feel clean. I feel less sorry.

I whisper, 'It's time for her to rest now.'

He says nothing at first, hands me a turquoise-coloured towel, and finally whispers, '*Allah y rahma.*'

I don't know how he understood what I was talking about. I stretch out on a brown couch stained with water rings and he serves me tea. Two large wall hangings separate the hammam from a small adjoining room. Coconut trees and a fine sandy beach. Upstairs, the manager is listening to the Quran. The voice blends with the faint jazz playing in the relaxation room. I finally fall asleep.

Pschschsch. Jolted awake by an automatic air freshener on the coffee table that went off ten centimetres from my ear. Drops of scented air land on my face. It's time to go.

I return to the apartment. It's brimming over, at least forty people. I'm nervous, but in fact it's amid the constant noise and everyone's annoying or telling or amusing mannerisms, surrounded by this huge extended family sprawling every which way, that my anxiety dissipates. The rooftop where my little cousins are playfighting, one in a wheelchair. The way it bumps against doorframes in rhythm with how much fun she's having. The joy splashing onto the food. The diversity and abundance of items that make it so that we have no idea where anything belongs anymore. People are forced to slouch against the walls, on pillows and rugs, but they do it with good-natured nonchalance. The haphazard organisation has disrupted habits, leaving the adults to eat on the floor. The kids are reading aloud, they stumbled on a book by Toni Morrison, the laughter flows. I feel clean. The chorus of voices and my cousins' peals of laughter sounds nice.

'Where were you?'
       'The hammam.'

For several days we do nothing. We go for walks, as a group, or sometimes I go on my own. I've only just got used to the narrow streets and the faces and it's time to go. I baulk. 'Our life is in France,' says my father. I look at him: migration is truly a psyche-splintering process. He seems happy here, really good here. Why leave? As for me, I don't know where my life is. I get the feeling I should listen more carefully to my joy at arriving and my sadness at leaving.

I get the feeling that I should think more carefully about a homecoming.

A taxi and a history lesson from my father about Ibn Battouta Airport. Customs. I'm asked, 'Anything to declare?'
       Me: 'Nothing. I mean . . . No, nothing.'

It's dumb, I don't know why I stammer. The man frowns. He's tall with a round face, like a ball screwed to a long thin neck. I'm taken into an adjacent room. It's the first time. This is when I understand the feeling, the one that comes over me when, from behind his desk, the Moroccan officer in his grey-green uniform asks me if I'm from here.

Where am I from?
    What's my connection to this country?
    Why is it that in my passport (my French passport), on the visa pages there are so many red and blue stamps for Tangiers, Marrakesh, Essaouira, Agadir . . .

He asks again and for the first time, I'm not irritated. I feel a swell of pride. I answer that it's my father, he's my connection to this country. I'd like to tell the officer everything, tell him about the others and the feeling of waste that comes after death.

Things get heated when he asks me, angrily, disdainfully, with cruel indifference, why I don't have my card.
    My ID card, mine, not the ones I've seen, that belong to my family, my aunts, my father. No, *my* card with my name and my face, my identity on a piece of paper.

I answer, 'I'm going to get one, soon, *inshallah*.'

He gives me a surly, officious smile, and I feel claimed. Finally, I've found the word: claimed. I'm wanted as an integrated, defined element of a country. I'm wanted as an Arab.

A country that avoided me, eluded me every morning, every day and every night that someone furrowed their brows when they looked at my mixed face. My face puckered by indecision, by ethnic uncertainty (what a terrible term, but that's what comes).

France doesn't want me. It has me, cruelly so. It owns me without a second thought, but now, here in this place, I'm being claimed.

Inside me, there's an explosion and calm. What private magic to feel this way in front of the customs officer, across from the person who records nationalities. Meaning, identities. Across from the men in grey-green who decide who can enter or leave, I now see that this place, this land, is necessary.

Obvious, though, isn't it? That the world is always, if we want it to be, a disaster or a true miracle.

The agent leaves, to search my luggage I assume. I stay alone in the office for a long time. In silence. I look at the king's portrait. I look at the clock with Paris time. He comes back and tells me, 'It's fine. You can go.'

I cross the hallway and return to freedom. My father is waiting in front of the customs area. I see the fear on his tensed mouth. I get closer and I see the halos of sweat on his shirt. I'm guessing my conversation with the policeman lasted a lot longer for him than it did for me.

He sighs very slowly. I can't make out his eyes behind his sunglasses. He takes a step towards me and says something inaudible in Arabic. There's a strong smell of sweat, this will be the smell of reconciliation. I have trouble understanding the Arabic. I tell myself it's not a big deal. Oh well.

We exchange smiles.

'I don't blame you at all anymore.'